SWARMING AROUND THE KILL

Everywhere Sc  **fleet were breaki** **they plunged into** **softness, wings a** **heat, delicate necks snapped,** **falling like silver tears in the night.**

The Veritechs were faring better, but columns of Invid were now on the ascent to deal out their own form of injustice.

They fell upon the hapless transports and command ships first, helping along nature's cruel reversal with deliberately placed rends and breaches, spreading further ruination throughout the fleet. Scott saw acts of bravery and futility: a Battloid, already crippled and falling backward into the atmosphere, pouring cannonfire against the enemy; two superheated Veritechs attempting to defend a transport against dozens of Invid claw fighters; another VT, boosters blazing, in a kamikaze run toward the head of the column.

Scott instructed his ship to jettison its rear augmentation pack and increased his speed, atmosphere be damned. There was still an outside chance that some of Gardner's crew had made it into the evacuation pods. If only the Invid could be kept away from the hapless transport.

"Please, pull out!" Scott was screaming through gritted teeth. "Please, please..."

The ROBETECH™ Series
Published by Ballantine Books:

ROBOTECH™ #10
INVID INVASION

Jack McKinney

A Del Rey Book

BALLANTINE BOOKS • **NEW YORK**

All rights reserved under International and Pan-American Copyright Conventions. Published in the United States of America by Ballantine Books, a division of Random House, Inc., New York, and simultaneously in Canada by Random House of Canada Limited, Toronto.

Library of Congress Catalog Card Number: 87-91487

ISBN 0-345-34143-0

Printed in Canada

First Edition: October 1987

Cover art by David Schleinkofer

PROLOGUE

SOMEWHERE A QUEEN WAS WEEPING...HER children scattered; her regent a prisoner of the blood lust, at war with nature and enslaved to vengeance.

But dare we presume to read her thoughts even now, to walk a path not taken—one denied to us by gates and towers our senses cannot perceive and perhaps never will?

Still, it must have seemed like the answer to a prayer: A planet newly rich in the flower that was life itself, a profusion of such incredible nutrient wealth that her Sensor Nebulae had found it clear across the galaxy. A blue and white world as distant from her Optera as she was from the peaceful form her consciousness once inhabited.

And yet Optera was lost to her, to half her children. Left in the care of one who had betrayed his

1

kind, who had become what he fought so desperately to destroy. As she herself had. . . .

All but trapped now in the guise that *he* had worn, the one who lured the secrets of the Flower from her. And whose giant warriors had returned to possess the planet and dispossess its inhabitants. *But oh, how she had loved him!* Enough to summon from her very depths the ability to emulate him. And later to summon a hatred keen enough to birth a warring nature, an army of soldiers to rival his—to rival *Zor's* own!

But he, too, was lost to her, killed by the very soldiers her hatred had fashioned.

Oh, to be rid of these dark memories! her ancient heart must have screamed. *To be rescued from these sorry realms!* Garuda, Spheris, Tirol. *And this Haydon IV with its sterile flowers long awaiting the caress of the Pollinators—this confused world even my Inorganics cannot subdue.*

But she was aware that all these things would soon be behind her. She would gather the cosmic stuff of her race and make the jump to that world the Sensor Nebulae had located. *And woe to the life-form that inhabited that world!* For nothing would prevent her from finding a home for her children, a home for the completion of their grand evolutionary design!

News of the Invid exodus from Haydon IV spread through the Fourth Quadrant—to Spheris and Gàruda and Praxis, worlds already abandoned by the insect-like horde, worlds singled out by fate to feel the backlash of Zor's attempt at recompense, nature's cruel joke.

The Tirolian scientist had attempted to foliate them with the same Flowers he had been ordered to steal from Optera, an action that had sentenced that warm world's sentient life-form to a desperate quest to relocate their nutrient grail. But Zor's experiments had failed, because the Flower of Life proved to be a discriminating plant—choosy about where it would and would not put down roots—and a malignantly loyal one as well.

Deriving as much from the Invid as the Invid derived from it, the Flower called out from Zor's seeded worlds to its former guardian/hosts. Warlike and driven—instincts born of the Robotech Masters' transgression—the Invid answered those calls. Their army of mecha and Inorganics arrived in swarms to overwhelm and rule; and instead of the Protoculture paradises the founder of Robotechnology had envisioned, were planets dominated by the beings his discoveries had all but doomed.

And now suddenly they were gone, off on a new quest that would take them clear across the galactic core.

To Earth . . .

Word of their departure reached Rick Hunter aboard the Sentinel's ships. He was in the command seat on the fortress bridge when the communiqué was received. Thin and pale, a war-weary veteran of countless battles, Rick was almost thirty-five years old by Earth reckoning, but the vagaries of hyperspace travel put him closer to fifty or two hundred and seventy, depending on how one figured it.

The giant planet Fantoma, once home to the Zentraedi, filled the forward viewports. In the foreground Rick could just discern the small inhabited moon called Tirol, an angry dot against Fantoma's barren face. *How could such an insignificant world have unleashed so much evil on an unsuspecting galaxy?* Rick wondered.

He glanced over at Lisa, who was humming to herself while she tapped a flurry of commands into her console. *His wife*. They had stayed together through thick and thin these past eleven years, although they had had their share of disagreements, especially when Rick had opted to join the Sentinels—Baldon, Teal, Crysta, and the others—and pursue the Invid.

Who would have thought it would come to this? he asked himself. A mission whose purpose had been peace at war with itself. Edwards and his grand designs of empire... how like the Invid regent he was, how like the Masters, too! But he was history now, and that fleet he had raised to conquer Earth would be used to battle the Invid when the Expeditionary Force reached the planet.

Providing the fleet reached Earth, of course. There were still major problems with the spacefold system Lang and the Tirolian Cabell had designed. Some missing ingredient... Major Carpenter had never been heard from, nor Wolff; and now the Mars and Jupiter Group attack wings were preparing to fold, with almost two thousand Veritechs between them.

Rick exhaled slowly and deliberately, loud enough for Lisa to hear him and turn a thin smile his way. Somehow it was fitting that Earth should end up on the Invid's list, Rick decided. But what could have happened there to draw them in such unprecedented numbers? Rick shuddered at the thought.

Perhaps Earth was where the final battle was meant to be fought.

Ravaged by the Robotech Masters and their gargantuan agents, the Zentraedi, it was a miracle that Earth had managed to survive at all. Looking on the planet from deep space, it would have appeared unchanged: its beautiful oceans and swirling masses of cloud, its silver satellite, bright as any beacon in the quadrant. But a closer look revealed the scars and disfigurations those invasions had wrought. The northern hemisphere was all but a barren waste, forested by the rusting remains of Dolza's ill-fated four-million-ship armada. Great cities of gleaming concrete, steel, and glass towers lay ruined and abandoned. Wide highways and graceful bridges were cratered and collapsed. Airports, schools, hospitals, sports complexes, industrial and residential zones... reduced to rubble, unmarked graveyards all.

A fifteen-year period of peace—that tranquil prologue to the Masters' arrival—saw the resurrection of some of those things the twentieth century had all but taken for granted. Cities had rebuilt themselves, new ones had grown up. But humankind was now a different species from that which had originally raised those towering sculptures of stone. Post-Cataclysmites, they were a feudal, warring breed, as distrustful of one another as they were of those stars their hopeful ancestors had once wished upon. Perhaps, as some have claimed, Earth actually called in its second period of catastrophe, as if bent on adhering to some self-fulfilling prophecy of doom. The Masters, too, for that matter: The two races met and engaged in an unspoken agreement for mutual annihilation—a paving of the way for what would follow.

Those who still wish to blame Protoculture trace the genesis of this back to Zor, Aquarian-age Prometheus, whose gift to the galaxy was a Pandora's box he willingly opened. Displaced and repressed, the Flower of Life had rebelled. And there were no chains, molecular or otherwise, capable of containing its power. That Zor, resurrected by the Elders of his race for their dark purposes, should have been the one to free the Flower from its Matrix is now seen as part of Protoculture's equation. Equally so, that that liberation should call forth the Invid to complete the circle.

They came without warning: a swarm of monsters and mecha folded across space and time by their leader/queen, the Regis, through an effort of pure psychic will. They did not choose to announce themselves the way their former enemies had, nor did they delay their invasion to puzzle out humankind's strengths and weaknesses, quirks and foibles. There was no need to determine whether Earth did or did not have what they sought; their Sensor Nebulae had already alerted them to the presence of the Flower. It had found compatible soil and climate on the blue and white world. All that was required were the Pollinators, a missing element in the Robotech Masters' equations.

In any case, the Invid had already had dealings with Earthlings, having battled them on a dozen planets, including Tirol itself. But as resilient as the Humans might have been on Haydon IV, Spheris, and the rest, they were a pathetic lot on their homeworld.

In less than a week the Invid conquered the planet, destroying the orbiting factory satellite—an ironic end for the Zentraedi aboard—laying to waste city after city, and dismissing with very little effort the vestiges of the Army of the Southern Cross. Depleted of the Protoculture charges necessary to fuel their Robo-technological war machines, those warriors who had fought so valiantly against the Masters were forced to fall back on a small supply of nuclear weapons and conventional ordnance that was no match for the Invid's plasma and laser-array superiority.

Even if Protoculture had been available to the

Southern Cross for their Hovertanks and Alpha Veritechs, there would have been gross problems to overcome: the two years since the mutual annihilation of the Robotech Masters and Anatole Leonard's command had seen civilization's unchecked slide into lawlessness and barbarism. Cities became city-states and warred with one another; men and women rose quickly to positions of power only to fall even more swiftly in the face of greater military might. Greed and butchery ruled, and what little remained of the northern hemisphere's dignity collapsed.

Though certain cities remained strong—Mannatan, for example (formerly New York City)—the centers of power shifted southward, into Brazilas especially (the former Zentraedi Control Zone), where growth had been sure and steady since the SDF-1's return to devastated Earth and the founding of New Macross and its sister city, Monument.

Unlike the Zentraedi or the Tirol Masters, the Invid were not inclined to destroy the planet or exterminate humankind. Quite the contrary: Not only had the Flower found favorable conditions for growth, the Invid had as well. The Regis had learned enough in her campaign against the Tirolians and the so-called Sentinels to recognize the continuing need for technology. Gone was the blissful tranquillity of Optera, but the experiment had to be carried forth to its conclusion nonetheless, and Earth was well suited for the purpose.

After disarming and occupying the planet, the Regis believed she was more than halfway toward her goal. By utilizing a percentage of Humans to cultivate and harvest the Flowers, she was free to carry out her experiments uninterrupted. The central hive, which came to be called Reflex Point, was to be the site of the Great Work, but secondary hives were soon in place across the planet to maintain control of the Human sectors of her empire. The Regis was willing to let humankind survive until such time as the work neared completion. Then, she would rid herself of them.

There was, however, one thing she had not taken into account: the very warriors she had fought tooth and claw on those worlds once seeded by Zor. Enslave a world she might, but take it for her own? *Never!*

CHAPTER
ONE

The armada of Robotech ships T.R. Edwards had amassed for his planned invasion and conquest of Earth would be put to that very use years later when Admiral Hunter sent them against the Invid. Adding irony to irony, it should be mentioned that the warships had serious design flaws which went unnoticed during their use on Tirol. Assuming this would have been the case even if Edwards had managed to persevere, the invasion would have failed. Destiny failed to deliver Edwards the crown he felt justified to wear and likewise failed to deliver Hunter the quick victory he felt justified to claim.

Selig Kahler, *The Tirolian Campaign*

A FLEET OF ROBOTECH WARSHIPS MOVED INTO ATtack formation above the Moon, a mixed school of gleaming predators, radiant where the distant sun touched their armored hulls and alloy fins. Each carried in its belly a score or more of Veritech fighters, sleek, transformable mecha developed and perfected over the course of the past thirty years. And inside each of these was a pilot ready to die for a world unseen. War was at the top of the agenda, but in a narrow hold aboard one of the command vessels a young man was thinking about love.

He was a pleasant-looking, clean-shaven youth going on twenty, with his father's long legs and the wide eyes of his mother. He wore his blue-black hair combed straight back from his high forehead—save for that undisciplined strand that always seemed to fall forward—making his ears appear more prominent than they actually were. He wore the Expeditionary Force uniform— simple gray tight-fitting pants tucked into high boots and a short-sleeved ornately collared top worn over a crimson-colored synthcloth bodysuit. The Mars Group patch adorned the young man's shirt.

His name was Scott Bernard—Lieutenant Scott Bernard—and this was a homecoming of sorts. That fact, coupled with the anxieties he felt concerning the imminent battle, had put him in an impassioned frame of mind. The fortunate recipient of this not-so-sudden desire was a pretty, dark-eyed teenager named Marlene, a good six inches shorter than Scott, with milk-chocolate-brown hair and shapely legs enhanced by the uniform's short skirt.

Scott had Marlene's small face cupped in his hands while he looked lovingly into her eyes. As his hands slid to her narrow shoulders, he pulled her to him, his mouth full against hers, stifling the protest her more cautious nature wished to give voice to and urging her to respond. Which she did, with a moan of pleasure, her hands flat against his chest.

"Marry me, Marlene," he said after she had broken off their embrace. He heard himself say it and almost applauded, simply for finally getting the nerve up to ask her; Marlene's response was a separate issue.

Her surprised gasp probably said the same: that *she* too couldn't believe he was finally getting around to it. She turned away from him, nervous hands at her chin in an attitude of prayer.

"Well, will you?" Scott pressed.

"It's a bit sudden," she said coyly. But Scott didn't pick up on her tone and reacted as though he had been slapped.

"You'll have to speak to my father first," Marlene continued in the same tone, her back to him still. "My mother, too." When she turned around, Scott was staring at her slack-jawed.

"But they're back on *Tirol*!" he stammered. "They might not be here for—" Then he caught her smile and understood at once. He had literally known her for her entire life, and he still couldn't tell when she was putting him on.

Marlene was smiling up at him now, eyes beaming. But the sudden shrill of sirens collapsed her happiness.

"Defold operation complete," a voice said over the PA. "All wing commanders report to the bridge for final briefing and combat assignments."

Scott's lips were a thin line when he looked at her.

"Answer me, Marlene. I might not get another chance to ask you."

The command ship bridge was a tight, no-nonsense affair, with two duty stations squeezed between the wraparound viewports and four more back to back behind these. There was none of the spaciousness and calm that had characterized the SDF-1 bridge; here everyone had a seat, and everyone put duty first. It took something like the first sight of Earth to elicit any casual conversation, and even then the comments would have surprised some.

"I'm so excited," a woman tech was saying. "I can hardly wait to see what Earth looks like after all these years."

Commander Gardner, seated at the forward station of starboard pair, heard this and laughed bitterly to himself. He had served under Gloval during the First Robotech War and had been with Hunter since. His thick hair and mustache had gone to silver these past few years, but he still retained a youthful energy and the unwavering loyalty of his young crew.

The woman tech who had spoken was all of seventeen years old, born in deep space like most of her shipmates. Gardner wished for a moment he could have showed her the Earth of forty years ago, teeming with life, wild and wonderful and blissfully unaware of the coming tide. . . .

"What does it matter?" the tech's male console mate answered her. "One planet's the same as another to me. Robotech ships are all I've known—all I want to know."

"Don't you have any interest in setting foot on your homeworld? Our parents were born here. And *their* parents, right on back to the first ancestors."

Gardner could almost hear the copilot's shrug of indifference clear across the bridge.

"Just another Invid colony, color it what you will. So this place is blue and Spheris was brown. It doesn't do anything for me."

"Spoken like a true romantic."

The copilot snorted. "You get romantic thinking about the Invid grubbing around the old homestead looking for Protoculture?"

Commander Gardner was hanging on the answer when the door to the bridge hissed open suddenly and Lieutenant Bernard entered.

"Alpha Group is just about ready for launch," Bernard reported.

Gardner muttered, "Good," and rose from the contoured seat, signaling one of the techs to turn on the ship's PA system.

"Most of you know what I'm about to say," he began. "But for those who don't know what this mission is all about, it's simply this: Several months ago we became aware that the Invid Sensor Nebulae had located some new and apparently enormous supply of the Flowers of

Life. The source of the transmissions turned out to be the Earth itself.

"The Regis moved quickly to secure the Flowers, with the same murderous intent she demonstrated on Spheris and Haydon IV and a dozen other worlds I don't have to remind you about. Nor should I have to remind you about what we're going to face on Earth. It seems probable that the Invid decimated Wolff's forces, but we number more than four times the units under his command."

Scott noticed that the bridge techs, eyes locked on Gardner and grim faces set, were giving silent support to the commander's words. Marlene entered the bridge in the midst of the briefing, whispering her apologies and seating herself at her duty station.

"Admiral Hunter has entrusted us to spearhead a vast military operation to invade and reclaim our home-world," said Gardner. "And I know that I can count on every one of you to stand firm behind the admiral's con-viction that we can lay the foundations for his second wave." He inclined his head. "May God have mercy on our souls."

A brief silence was broken by the navigator's update:

"Earth orbit in three minutes, Commander. Placing visual display on the monitor, sir."

Everyone turned to face the forward screen. Orbital schematics de-rezzed and were replaced by a full view of the Earth. They had all seen photos and video images galore, but the sight inspired awe nevertheless.

"It's beautiful," someone said. And compared to Fan-toma or Tirol, it most certainly was: snow-white pole, blue oceans, and variegated land masses, the whole of it patterned by swirling clouds.

A computer-generated grid assembled itself over the image as the command ship continued to close. At her station, Marlene said, "So that's what Earth looks like . . . I'd almost forgotten."

The commander called for scanning to be initiated, and in a moment the grid was highlighting an area located in one of the northern continents. Data readouts scrolled across an adjacent display screen.

"Full magnification and color enhancement," Gardner barked.

Marlene leaned in to study her screen. The forward monitor was displaying an angry red image, not softened in the least by Earth's inviting cloud cover. She knew what this was but asked the computer to compare the present readings with those logged in its memory banks. She sensed that Scott was peering over the top of her high-backed chair.

"That's it, sir," she said all at once, her screen strobing encouragement. "The central hive. Designation... Reflex Point," Marlene read from the data scroll. "Picking up energy flux readings and multiple radar contacts... waiting for signature."

Gardner glanced over at her briefly, then turned his attention forward once again. "I want visuals as soon as possible," he instructed one of the techs.

"Shock Trooper transport," Marlene said at the same time.

Gardner's nostrils flared. "Prepare to repel."

Techs were already bending over the consoles tapping in commands, the bridge a veritable light show of flashing screens.

"Two minutes to contact," the navigator informed Gardner.

"All sections standing by..."

"Auto-astrogator is off... Ship's shields raised..."

Marlene flipped a series of switches. "Net is open...."

"All right," Gardner said decisively. "Issue the go signal to all Veritechs."

"One minute and counting, sir..."

The commander turned to Scott.

"It's up to your squads now, Lieutenant. We've got to get through their lines and set these ships down." Scott saluted, and Gardner returned it. "Good luck," he added.

"You can count on us."

Marlene had turned from her station, waiting for him to walk past. As he leaned down to kiss her, she smiled and surprised him by placing a heart-shaped holo-locket into his hand.

"Take this with you," she said while he was regarding the thing. "It's my way of saying 'good luck.'"

Scott thanked her and leaned in to collect that kiss after all. Resurfaced, he found Gardner and the techs smiling at him; he gave another crisp salute and rushed from the bridge.

"'Good-bye, sweetheart,'" one of the techs stationed behind Marlene mimicked not a moment after Scott left. "'And here's a token of my undying love.'"

Marlene poked her head around the side of the chair. Marf and one who liked to be called Red were laughing. "Knock it off," she told them. She was used to the razzing—personal time was hard to come by aboard ship, and Scott's open displays of affection only added fuel to the fire—but in no mood for it right now.

"What's the matter, Marlene?" Red said over his shoulder. "Don't you know that absence makes the heart grow fonder?"

She swiveled about in the cushioned seat and hid her face in her hands. "I don't know how it could," she managed, suddenly on the verge of tears.

"Don't let them get to you, Marlene," one of her supporters at the forward stations called out while Red laughed.

Come back, Scott, she prayed. *I'd give my life to keep you safe.*

* * *

Gardner's command ship was actually one of the fleet's many transport vessels—delicate-looking ships that resembled swans in flight, with long, tapering necks and thin swept-back wings under each of which was affixed a boxcarlike Veritech carrier.

Scott, his body sheathed in lime-green armor, was strapping himself into one of the Veritechs now. Fifteen years had seen only minor changes in armor and craft. Lang's Robotech design team had maintained the "thinking caps" and sensor-studded mitts and boots that were so characteristic of the first-generation VT pilots. Armor itself had become somewhat bulky due to the fact that these third-generation warriors were involved in ground-assault missions as often as they were in space strikes; but there was none of the gladiatorial styling favored by Lang's counterparts in the Army of the Southern Cross.

"The main engine and boosters are in top shape, sir," a launch tech perched on the rim of the Veritech bin told Scott before he lowered the canopy. "Good luck and good hunting."

Scott flashed him a thumbs-up as the canopy sealed itself. "Thanks, pal," he said over the externals. "I'll be seein' you Earthside."

Flashes of green and red light from the cockpit displays played across the tinted faceshield of Scott's helmet as he activated and engaged one after another of the Veritech's complex systems. "This is Commander Bernard of the Twenty-first Armored Tactical Assault Squadron, Mars Division," he announced over the com net. "Condition is green, and we are go for launch."

"The flight bay is open," control radioed back to him. "You are cleared for launch, Commander."

Scott gave a start as bay doors throughout the carrier retracted. The cloud-studded deep-blue oceans of Earth filled his entire field of vision. The sight elicited a sense

of vertigo he had never experienced before; it was difficult for him to comprehend a planet with so much water,
a liquid world that offered so little surface.... But Scott
was quick to catch himself.

"Mars Division attack wing," he said over the net,
"let's do it!"

The Veritech lurched somewhat as the bin conveyers
began to move the fighters toward the forward bay. Scott
saw that the grappler pylons that would convey the
mecha from belt to vacuum had already attached themselves. He readied himself at the controls, urging his
body to relax, his mind to meld with the VT systems. In
a moment he felt the grapplers release, the fighter drifting weightlessly, before he engaged the thrusters that
bore it away from the transport carrier.

"All right, look alive," Scott said as his wingmen
came alongside to signal their readiness. "Once we join
up with the main formation, I want eyes open and hands
on the trigger." Earthspace was filled with mecha now,
some two thousand Veritechs in a slow descent over a
silent world. Scott heard Commander Gardner's voice
over the com net.

"All wing commanders maintain loose battle formation.... prepare to break off for individual combat
at the first sign of enemy hostility. It shouldn't be long
in coming...."

It is unlikely that many of the men and women who
made up the Mars Division (so named by Dr. Lang to
convey a sense of attachment to Earth and its brethren
worlds) recognized the uniqueness of their position:
Their invasion represented humankind's first *deliberate*
offensive against an XT force. Up to that point Earth
had always been on the defensive, counterstriking first
the Zentraedi, then those giants' Tirolian Masters, and
lastly (and unsuccessfully) the Invid themselves. In this
sense the day was a red-letter event, if not the turn-

ing point Hunter and numerous others had all hoped it would be. . . .

Scott was one of the first to see the enemy ship; it was below him at nine o'clock, surfacing through Earth's atmosphere at an alarming rate. An Invid troop carrier, one of the so-called Mollusk Carriers.

"Here they are," Scott said to his wingmen, gesturing with his hand at the same time. The clamshell-shaped fortress was yawning now, revealing an arena array of Invid Shock Trooper mecha. "Fall in on my signal."

When Scott looked again a split second later, an Invid column launched itself and was locked in on an ascent to engage, the ships' crablike hulls and pincer arms a gleaming golden-brown in Sol's intense light. "Yeah, I think we're gonna see signs of hostility," Scott muttered to himself as his squadron dropped in to meet the enemy at the edge of space.

At Scott's command the pilots of the Twenty-first thumbed off flocks of heat-seeker missiles, which streaked into the ascending column. Short-lived explosions of violent light blossomed against Earth's blue and white backdrop. The VTs continued their silent descents, loosing second and third salvos of red-tipped demons against that horde which had overwhelmed their world. And countless Invid mecha flamed out and fried, but not enough to matter. For every one taken out there were three that survived, and those which broke through the line of fire began to strike back. Scott knew there were creatures inside each of those ships—huge bipedal mockeries of the Human form, with massive arms and heads that resembled elongated snouts.

Unlike the enemy forces of the First and Second Robotech Wars, the Invid relied on numbers rather than firepower. True, the Zentraedi had a seemingly endless supply of Battlepods and an armada of ships four million strong, but by and large the war was fought in conventional terms. Up against the Masters this was even more the case, with the number of mecha on both sides substantially reduced. With the Invid, however, humankind encountered a horde mentality to rival any that nature had produced. And true to form, whether army ants or swarms of killer bees, the Invid carried a sting.

As Scott and the others knew from their previous encounters, initial fusillades were what counted most. Once separated from its column, the individual Invid ship was blindingly maneuverable and often unstoppable. In close it favored two approaches: ripping open mecha with its alloy pincer claws and embracing a ship and literally shocking it to death with charges delivered by the ships' Protoculture systems. Scott saw both variations of this occurring while he did his best to keep his own fighter out of reach.

Veritech and crabship were going at it across the field, Mars Division troops and Invid mecha in deadly pursuits and dogfights, crisscrossing in the upper reaches of the stratosphere amidst tracer rounds, missile tracks, and laser-array fire from the command ships. Scott saw one of his team taken out by a claw swipe that opened the Veritech tail to nose, precious atmosphere sucked from the fractured canopy, the pilot flailing for life inside. In another part of nearby space, several Veritechs floated derelict after loveless Invid embraces.

Scott realized the hopelessness of their situation and ordered his squadron to reconfigure to Battloid mode.

Mechamorphosis, or mode selection, was still controlled by a three-position cockpit lever, along with the pilot's mecha will, which interfaced with the fighter's Protoculture-governed systems. But where all parts of the first-generation Veritechs participated in reconfiguration, the augmentation packs and energy generators of the Armored Alphas (essential for the space and ground missions that typified the Expeditionary Force) remained intact during the process. The forward portion of the craft telescoped to accomplish this, arms unfolding from behind the canopy while radome and cockpit rotated up through a 180-degree arc, now allowing the underbelly laser turret to become the Battloid's head, and the underbelly rifle/cannon to become the weapon that was grasped in the mecha's right hand.

Thus transformed, Scott's squadron fell in to reengage the Invid, blue thrusters bright in Earth's dark side.

Meanwhile, a second wave of Veritechs was launched from the transports to respond to another column of Invid approaching swiftly from Delta sector.

Scott's displays flashed coordinates and signatures of the second Mollusk Carrier even before he had visual contact. He ordered his team to form up on his lead and throw themselves against the column. Once again heat-seekers found their marks and took out scores of Invid ships; and once again orange hell-flowers blossomed. But reinforced, the Invid launched a frenzied counter-strike. Shock vessels broke through the front lines and went for the transports themselves in suicide runs and massed charges. Particle beams, disgorged from bow guns, swept like insecticide through their ranks, annihilating ship after ship.

Scott's team regrouped and gave chase to any that survived, blasts from the VTs' chain-guns blowing pincers to debris and holing carapaces. Still, Scott could hear the death screams of the unlucky ones piercing the tac net's cacophony of commands and reactions. VTs and Invid ships drifted from the arena, locked in bizarre postures, obscene embraces. Here, an Invid pincer was apparently caught in the canopy of the ship it had ensnared; there, another held a VT to itself, exchanging lightning flashes of death.

Scott, sweat beading up across his forehead, was in pursuit of two Invid ships that were closing in on Commander Gardner's transport; he had heard Marlene's terror-stricken call for help only a moment before and had one of the enemy ships bracketed in the chain-gun's sights now. He fired once, shooting a hole through its groin, and smiled devilishly as it disintegrated in a brief burst of crimson light. The second Invid, its pincers raised for action, was moving toward the bridge viewports. But fire from Scott's cannon decommissioned it before it attained striking distance.

"Saw two, swatted same," Scott told Marlene over the com net, a confident tone returned to his voice. The Invid were falling back on all sides.

"Good job, Commander," Gardner congratulated him before Marlene had a chance to speak. "Signal your team to begin their atmospheric approach. Our thermal energy shields are already seriously drained."

"Roger," said Scott, at the same time waving the chain-gun to signal his wingmen. "We'll escort you through."

Scott saw the transport's thrusters fire a three-second burst, realigning the ship for its slow descent. He sat back and punched up orbital entry calculations on the data screen, fed these over to the autopilot, and returned his attention to wide-range radar. Suddenly Marlene was on the net again, alerting him to a unit of bandits moving against him at four o'clock. He glanced over his shoulder and glimpsed them even as their signatures were registering on the mecha's radar screen.

"I see them," he answered her calmly.

Scott permitted the half dozen Invid to close in, enabling his onboard targeting computer to get a fix on all of them. It was a calculated risk but one that paid off a moment later when the Battloid's deltoid compartments opened and each launched a missile that homed in on its target. Scott boostered himself away from the silent fireworks and rechecked the screen: There was no sign of enemy activity.

"We're all clear, Commander," he reported, easing up the thinking cap's faceshield.

Gardner's face now flashed into view on the cockpit's small commo screen. "Scott! We must try to slip through and hit Reflex Point before the Regis's drones have a chance to regroup. Understood?"

"Roger Commander," Scott returned. At a signal from the HUD, he dropped the faceshield, the inside surface of which was displaying approach vectors and numerical data. He opened the tac net. "Our entrance azimuth is one-two-one-one . . . Reconfiguring for orbital deviation."

Scott armed the Veritech's shield after it had shifted mode and brought the fighter alongside Gardner's descending transport. The hull temperature of his own ship was reaching critical levels, and he reasoned that the same thing had to be occurring on the larger ship. A glance told him he was correct and more. The underside of the command vessel was radiating an intense glow that suggested an improper angle of approach. Scott waited for the vessel to correct itself, and when it didn't, he went on the net.

"Recommend you recalculate entry horizon, Commander. The ship appears to be entering too quickly."

"It can't be helped, Scott. We've got to put down. Our shields will never see us through another attack."

"Sir, you'll never live to see another attack if you don't readjust your course heading," Scott said more firmly. "That ship wasn't built for this kind of gravitational pull. You're going to tear her apart!"

Scott tried to suppress a mounting feeling of panic. He heard Marlene tell Gardner that the reserve thermal energy shields were now completely exhausted. Gardner ordered her to engage the retros.

Scott craned his neck to see if the retros were having any effect, his guts like a knot pressing against his diaphragm. He saw something break free from the tail section of the transport, glow, and burn out. He was trying to maintain proximity with the ship, but as a result his own displays were suddenly flashing warnings as well. *I'd better slow down myself if I don't want to be decorating a big part of the landscape.*

Scott pulled the mode selector to G position and stepped out of his fear temporarily to think the Veritech through to Guardian mode. As the legs of the mecha dropped, reverse-articulating, he engaged the foot thrusters, substantially cutting his speed. At the same time, Gardner's transport was roaring past him in an uncontrolled plunge.

"Commander, pull out!" he cried into the net. *Marlene!*

Caught between self-sacrifice and desperation, Scott could do little more than bear witness to the agonizingly slow deterioration of the command ship—the end of all he held dear in the world. The transport was a glowing ember now, slagging off fragments of itself into the void. The intense heat would have already boiled the blood of those inside....

Marlene!

His mind tried to save him from the horror by denying the events, cocooning him in much the same way the Veritech did. But averting his gaze only worsened matters: Everywhere he looked ships-of-the-fleet were breaking apart, flaming out as they plunged into Earth's betraying blue softness, wings and stabilizers folded by heat, delicate necks snapped, molten alloy falling like silver tears in the night.

The Veritechs were faring better, but columns of Invid were now on the ascent to deal out their own form of injustice.

They fell upon the helpless transports and command ships first, helping nature's cruel reversal along with deliberately placed rends and breaches, spreading further ruin throughout the fleet. Scott saw acts of bravery and futility: a Battloid already crippled and falling backward into the atmosphere pouring cannon fire against the enemy; two superheated Veritechs attempting to defend a transport against dozens of Invid claw fighters; another VT, boosters blazing, in a kamikaze run toward the head of the column.

Scott instructed his ship to jettison the rear augmentation pack and increased his speed, atmosphere be damned. There was still an outside chance that some of Gardner's crew had made it into the evacuation pods. If only the Invid could be kept away from the hapless transport.

"Please, pull out!" Scott was screaming through gritted teeth. "Please, please..."

Then, all at once, the transport's triple-thrusters died out, and an instant later the ship was engulfed in a soundless fireball that blew it to pieces.

Marlene! Scott railed at the heavens, his fists striking blows against the canopy and console as the Veritech commenced a swift unguided fall.

TWO

I don't think I'll ever forget the first time I laid eyes on Scott Bernard—beneath all that Robotech armor, I mean. He had the Look of the Lost in his eyes, and a stammer in his voice that was pure tremolo. The latter proved to be a case of offworld accent—some Tirolian holdover—but that Look . . . I just couldn't meet his eyes; I sat there tinkering with the Cyclone, trying to figure out whether I should run for the hills or off the guy then and there. Later on—much later on—he told me about that first night in the woods. I've got to laugh, even now: Ask Scott Bernard the one about the tree falling in the wilderness—and prepare to have your head bitten off!

Rand, *Notes on the Run*

TIROL, ONCE THE HOMEWORLD OF THE ROBOTECH Masters, then an Invid colony when the Masters had uprooted the remnants of their dying race and journeyed to Earth in search of Protoculture, was a reconfigured planet, much of its surface given over to humankind's needs, its small seas and weather patterns tamed. Not like this Earth, Scott thought, with its solitary yellow sun and distant silver satellite. He yearned for Tirol. It had been his home as much as the SDF-3 had been; he missed the binary stars of Fantoma's system, the protective presence of the motherworld itself. *How remote one felt from the heavens on this displaced world.*

Scott recalled Admiral Hunter's rousing send-off speech, his talk of the "cool green hills of home"—his home, Earth. Scott laughed bitterly to himself, the planet's native splendor lost on him.

The Alpha had found a soft spot to cushion its fall in some sort of highland forest. Oak and fir trees, Scott guessed. The VT was history, but cockpit harnesses and collision air bags had kept him in one piece. However, the crash had been violent enough to plow up a large hunk of the landscape. He had lost his helmet and sustained a forehead bruise; then came a follow-up thigh wound of his own making when he had rather carelessly climbed from the wreck.

He was sitting in the grass now, his back against the fighter's fuselage, his head and left leg bandaged with gauze from the ship's first-aid kit. He had gotten rid of his cumbersome armor just before nightfall but kept his blaster within reach.

The forest was dark and full of sounds he could not identify, although he was certain these were all *natural* calls and chirps and whistles—from what he had seen thus far, Earth was primitive and uncontrolled.

And there were just too many places for an enemy to hide.

"Give me a scorched Martian desert any day," Scott muttered.

He heard a rustling sound in the brush nearby and reached out for the blaster—a discette-shaped weapon developed on Tirol that was a scaled-down version of the one carried by the Masters' Bioroids during the Second Robotech War.

"Is there somebody out there?" he asked of the dark.

When the movement suddenly increased, he fired off a charge; it impacted with a blinding orange flash against a tree, flushing two small long-eared creatures from the undergrowth. Scott mistook them for Optera cha-chas at first—the Flower of Life Pollinators—then realized that they were rabbits.

What's happening to me? he asked himself, shaken by the cold fear that coursed through him. *Marlene and everything I loved destroyed, and now I'm losing my nerve.* He set the blaster aside and put his gloved hands to his face. It was possible he had sustained a concussion during the crash. A delayed onset of shock . . .

Lifting his head, he found that Earth had another surprise in store for him: The sky was dumping droplets of water on him—it was *raining*! Scott got up and walked to a clearing in the woods. He had heard about this phenomenon from old-timers but hadn't expected to encounter it. Scott could see that rain might not be a bad thing under certain conditions, but right now it was only adding to his discomfort. Besides, there was something else in the air that had come in with the rain: periods of a short-lived, rolling, explosive roar.

Clouds backlit by flashes of electrical charge were moving swiftly, obscuring the Moon and plunging the world into an impenetrable dark. Soon the angry bolts responsible for that stroboscopic light were overhead, launched like fiery spears toward the land itself, ear-splitting claps of thunder in their wake.

Scott found himself overwhelmed by a novel form of terror, so unlike the fear he was accustomed to that he stood screaming into the face of it, his feet seemingly rooted to the ground. This had nothing to do with enemy laser fire or plasma annihilation discs; it had nothing to do with combat or close calls. This was a larger terror, a deeper one, springing from an archaic part of himself he had never met face to face.

Unnerved, he ran for the safety of the Veritech cockpit as lightning struck and ignited one of the trees, toppling it with a second bolt that split the forest giant along its length. He lowered the canopy and hunkered down in the VT seat, hugging himself for warmth and security. Eyes tightly shut, ears filled with crackling noise, he shouted to himself: *What am I doing on this horrible planet?*

As if answering him, his mind reran images of the command ship's fiery demise, that slow and silent fatality.

"Marlene," he said through tears.

His hand had found the holo-locket she had given him on the bridge. But his forefinger was frozen on the activation button, his mind fearful of confronting the ghosts the device was meant to summon up. Still, he knew that he had to force himself to see and hear her again... before he could let the past die.

The metallic green heart opened at his touch, unfolding like a triptych; from its blood-red holo-bead center wafted a phantom image of Marlene.

"Scott, my darling, I know it isn't much, but I thought you'd get a kick out of this trinket. I'm looking forward to living the rest of my life with you. I can't wait till this conflict is all behind us. Till we meet again, my love..."

The voice that had been Marlene's trailed off, and the shimmering message returned to its place of captivity. Scott closed the heart and clutched it tightly in his fist, wishing desperately that he could so easily de-rezz the images held fast in his own heart. Outside, the storm continued unabated, echoing the dark night of his soul. Lighting fractured the alien sky, and rainwater ran in a steady stream across the protective curve of the VT's canopy.

In the morning Earth's skies seemed as blue as the seas Scott had seen from space; the air smelled sweet, washed clean of last night's violence. But this was little consolation. Fear and sorrow had lulled him into a fitful sleep, and the stark images of Marlene's death were with him when he awoke.

At a clear stream near the crash site, he filled his canteens with water. Taking in morning's soft light, the spectacle of the forest itself, the profusion of bird life, he suspected that Earth could be a tolerable place, after all, but doubted that he would ever feel at home here. He promised himself that he would turn his thoughts to the mission and only the mission from this point on. Insanity was the only alternative.

He returned to the Veritech and stowed the canteens with the survival gear he had already retrieved from the mecha. He had enough emergency rations to last him the better part of an Earth week; if he didn't come across a settlement or city by then, he would be forced to forage for food. And given what little information he had about edible plants and such, the thought was hardly an appetizing one.

He turned his attention now to the one item that was likely to rescue him from edible plants or privation: the Cyclone vehicle stored away in the fighter's small cargo compartment. A well-concealed sensor panel in the fuselage gave him access to this, and in a moment he was lifting the self-contained Cyclone free of the cargo hold. In its present collapsed state the would-be two-wheeled transport was no larger than a foot locker, but reconfigured it was equivalent to a 1,000-cc twentieth-century motorcycle. Which in fact it was, after a fashion.

Originally one of Robotechnology's first creations, it had undergone some radical modifications under Lang's SDF-3 teams. The Expeditionary Force had come to rely upon the vehicle as much as it had on the Veritech fighters, even though its design was still a basic one: a hybrid piston and Protoculture-powered transformable motorcycle that was a far cry from the Hovercycles developed on Earth during the same time period. Unlike that Southern Cross marvel, the Cyclone required the full interaction of its pilot, whose "thinking cap" and specially designed armor were essential to the functioning of the vehicle's Protoculture-based mechamorphic systems. In addition, it was light enough to carry, and wondrously fuel-efficient.

Scott carried the Cyclone several feet from the fighter and set about reconfiguring it, which entailed little more than flipping the appropriate switches. That much accomplished, he transferred his survival gear to the cycle's rear deck and began to struggle into the mecha's modular battle armor—not unlike the shoulder pads, hip harnesses, and leg and forearm protectors worn by turn-of-the-century athletes, except for the fact that the armor had been fashioned from lightweight alloys.

Scott was wearing Marlene's holo-heart around his neck now and gave a last look at it before snapping the armor's pectorals in place. *It's time, my love,* he said to the heart.

Again he told himself to concentrate on the mission. He recalled Commander Gardner's words: *If only one of you survive the invasion, you must locate the Invid Reflex Point and destroy it along with their queen, the Regis.* Scott had no idea how many people from Mars Division had survived atmospheric entry, but it was unlikely that any of them had touched down near his crash site. He had been so caught up in the destruction of the command ship that he had failed to lock the proper coordinates into the VT's autopilot. As a consequence, the mecha had surely delivered him far from any of the dozen preassigned rendezvous points and who knew how far from the Reflex Point itself. The stars told Scott that he had come down somewhere in the southern hemisphere, which put thousands of miles between him and the Regis if he was lucky, oceans between them if not. In any case, north was the direction of choice.

Scott donned his helmet and mounted the Cyclone. A thumb switch brought the mecha to life; he found his confidence somewhat restored by the throaty, synchronous firing of the cycle's systems.

Now let's get on with evening the score with the Regis and her Invid horde, Scott said to himself as he set off.

The worst thing about being a lone survivor were the memories that survived with you, Scott decided. If only one could erase them, switch them off somehow. But Scott knew that he couldn't; the people one loved were more frightening ghosts than anything imagination could conjure up. And they couldn't be outrun. . . .

Less than an hour from his crash site, Scott was surprised to find himself on what appeared to be a trail or an ancient roadway lined with trees. But an even greater shock awaited him over the rise: a veritable desert at the foot of the wooded foothills that witnessed his crash, stretching out toward distant barren mountains. Scott slid the Cyclone to a halt and stared homesick at the sight.

Who said there were no Fantoma landscapes on Earth?

Scott had never heard Wolff, Edwards, or any of the old-timers brag about this. It was almost as vast as Spheris!

Now reassured as well as renewed, Scott twisted the Cyclone's throttle and streaked down into the wastes.

Elsewhere in the wastes rode a survivor of a different campaign; but his cycle was of a different sort, (twenty years old if it was a day, and running desperately short of fuel pellets).

A clear-eyed, short, sinewy teenager with a shaggy mop of red hair and an unwashed look about him—both by necessity and by design—he called himself Rand, his inherited names long abandoned. He was born about the time the SDF-3 had been launched from Little Luna, and he had seen the rise and fall of Chairman Moran's government, the invasion of the Robotech Masters, and humankind's subsequent regression to barbarism, a turn of events that had culminated with the arrival of the Invid and their easily won conquest.

Just now Rand was doing what he did best: keeping himself alive. His old bike was closing in on the object he had seen plummet from the night sky two days ago, something too slow and controlled to have been a meteor, too massive for an Alpha. He had made up his mind to track its fall, abandoning his earlier plans to try for Laako City in the hopes of beating other Spotters, Foragers, and assorted rogues to the find.

Rand relaxed his wrist and let the bike come to a slow stop a good kilometer from the impact point. He threw back the hood of his shirt and slid his goggles up onto his forehead. The ship was even larger than he had guessed, like some great bird with enormous hexagonally shaped cargo pods strapped to the undersides of its wings. It was still glowing in places but obviously had been cooled by the rains that had drenched the irradiated wastes during the night. Rand cautiously resumed his forward motion, completing a circle around the thing at the same safe distance. There were no tracks or footprints in the still-moist sands, which meant that no one had left or entered the wreck during the past twelve hours or so.

He cycled through a second, tighter circle and headed in, convinced that he was first to arrive on the scene. Approaching the ship now, he could discern numbers and letters stenciled on the fuselage—M__R__ DIV____I____—but could make no sense of the whole —where it had come from or why.

The wreck had the stench of recent death written all over it. He wasn't in the least looking forward to walking into cargo bays wallpapered with Human remains, but he was just going to have to shut his eyes to that part of it.

There had to be something he could use, weapons or foodstuffs.

He began to circle the ship on foot now, searching for some way to get inside. The nose was throwing off so much heat there was no getting near it, but the rear hatch of one of the cargo carriers had sprung open on impact, and the place seemed cool enough to enter.

Rand threw himself atop the twisted wreck of the hatch and started in. The interior was dark and uninviting, and it smelled like hell. He knew he wasn't going to get very far, but not fifty feet into the thing—after whacking his head on a low threshold and falling flat on his face in the dark—he found more than enough to satisfy him: a bin of ten Robotech cycles.

He lifted one up and out of its rack and bent down to look it over. It was Robotech, all right, probably one of the Cyclone type the military had used before the development of the Hovercrafts. Rand had heard about them but never thought he would live to see one—let alone *ride* one!

Straddling the mecha now, he depressed the ignition switch, fingers of his left hand crossed for luck. The Cyclone fired, purring like a kitten, after a goose or two of the throttle.

"Awwriight!" Rand shouted.

He flicked on the headlight, screeched the Cyclone through a 360, and tore back toward the doorway, launching himself into the desert air from the sprung hatchway. He hit the sand and twisted the cycle to a halt, exhilarated from his short flight.

Then he noticed something else in flight: a three-unit Invid scouting party coming fast over a ridge of low hills to the west. Rand cursed himself for not figuring them into the picture; they, too, must have been aware of the transport's crash. And as always, their timing was impeccable. Even so, Rand was thankful that they were only Scouts and not Shock Troopers. In fact there was a good chance that the Cyclone would be able to outrun them—at least as far as the forest.

The three Scouts put down next to the downed ship, positioning themselves to prevent Rand's escape, the cloven foot of one them flattening the old cycle that had seen him through so much.

"I sure hope your insurance is paid up, pal!" Rand yelled at the Scout.

They were twenty-foot-tall bipedal creatures with articulated armored legs and massive pincer arms; there was no actual head, but raised egg-shaped protrusions atop their inverted triangular torsos were suggestive of eyes, while what looked to be a red-rimmed lipless mouth concealed a single sensor lens. Rand had seen brown ones and purple ones—these three were of the latter category—and more than anything they reminded him of two-legged land crabs. The Scouts were just that and were weaponless, except if one counted their innate repulsiveness. However, they could inflict serious damage with their claws, and just now one of the Scouts wanted to demonstrate that fact to Rand.

Rand shot the Cyclone forward at the Scout's first swipe, its claw striking the sand with a loud crunching sound. "Okay, but I'm going to be submitting a bill for damages!" he called over his shoulder as a second creature gave pursuit.

Rand's previous questions concerning the Cyclone's capabilities were soon to be answered. The three Invid were gaining on him, and ready or not he was going to have to put the cycle through its paces. He took a deep breath and kicked in the turbochargers. Instantaneously the Cyclone took off like a shot, living up to its namesake while Rand struggled to retain control. The Scouts meanwhile gave up their ground-shaking run and took to the air, thrusters carrying them overhead, pincer arms poised for the embrace that killed.

Their prey, however, had managed to overcome his initial ineptitude and was now leaning the Cyclone through a series of self-imposed twists and turns along the featureless sands, a tactic that more than once brought the Scouts close to midair collisions with one another.

"Just lemme know if you're gettin' tired!" Rand shouted above the roar of the mecha. He laughed over his shoulder and threw the Scouts a maniacal grin; but when he turned again to face front, he found trouble ahead. Something was approaching him fast, kicking up one heck of a dust storm. Two of the Invid were moving into flanking position, and it suddenly occurred to Rand that he would soon be surrounded.

Scott Bernard felt two emotions vying for his attention when he saw the Cyclone rider and the Invid Scouts: elation that he had found one of his Mars Division comrades and rage at the sight of the enemy. He couldn't figure out why the rider wasn't reconfiguring but knew that the situation called for immediate action. Lowering the helmet visor, he engaged the mecha's turbos. For a moment the Cyclone was up on its rear wheel, then it went fully airborne. At the same time, Scott's mind instinctively found the vibe that allowed it to inferface with the cycle's Protoculture systems.

Helped along by the imaging Scott's mind fed the Cyclone via the helmet "thinking cap," the mecha began to reconfigure. The windscreen and helmet assembly flattened out; the front wheel disengaged itself from the axle and swung back and off to one side. The rear wheel, along with most of the thruster pack, rode up, while other components, including the wheel-mounted missile tubes, attached themselves to Scott's hip, leg, and forearm armor. In the final stage of mechamorphosis, he resembled some kind of airborne armored backpacker whose gear just happened to include two solid rubber tires and a jet pack.

Scott let the thruster carry him in close to the Invid Scouts before bringing his forearm weapons into play—twin launch tubes that carried small but deadly Scorpion missiles. Right arm outstretched now, palm downward, he raised the tubes' targeting mechanism, centered one of the Scouts in the reticle, and loosed both missiles. They streaked toward their quarry with a deadly sibilance (Scott's armor protecting him from their backlash), narrowly missed Rand, and caught the Invid ship square in the belly, scattering pieces of it across the sands.

The unarmored Cyclone rider went down into a long slide while Scott took to the ground to dispatch his remaining pursuers. Once in their midst, he dodged two claw swipes before launching himself over the top of his would-be assailant. Another missed swipe and a second leap landed him atop one of the pair; he leapt up again and came down for the kill, firing off a single Scorpion from the left forearm launch tubes. While the Invid was engulfed by the ensuing explosion, Scott put down to deal with the last of them.

The thing tried to crush him with its foot, but Scott rolled away from it in time. Likewise, he dodged a right claw and jumped up onto the Invid's head. The Scout brought its left up now, almost in a gesture of puzzlement, but Scott was already gone. He toyed with the Invid for a minute more, allowing it another shot at him before polishing it off with the remaining Scorpion, which the Scout took right through its red optic scanner.

The Cyclone rider was still on the ground beneath his overturned mecha when Scott approached. "They're not really as tough as they look, are they?" he said to the bewildered red-haired civilian.

"*Hombre*, you're really something else in a battle," the man returned, his bushy eyebrows arched.

Scott raised the faceshield of his helmet. "The Cyclone does the work," he said humbly.

"Yeah, it's quite a rig," said Rand. He got up, dusted himself off, and righted the cycle, marveling at it once again. "You are a Forager?" he asked Scott warily. "Some kinda one-man army?"

"You might say that," Scott began. "Now listen—"

"It's the first time I ever actually rode one of these things!" Rand interrupted.

"I need some information—"

"I'll bet I could modify this to go twice the speed!" Rand was on his knees now, fidgeting with this and that. "Look at this control setup! I can't wait to try to reconfigure it!"

"Just where the hell are we, outlaw?" Scott managed at last. But when even that failed to elicit a response, he reached over the Cyclone and grabbed Rand by the shirtfront. "I'm talking to you, pal. Where'd those Scouts come from? Is there an Invid hive around here?"

Rand began to struggle against the mecha's hold, and Scott let him go. He was a scrappy kid but might make a decent partner.

Rand backed off, arms akimbo. "What do I look like, some kind of travel agent? I don't make a habit of asking them where they hail from—you just look up and there they are. I hate those things!"

"Take it easy," Scott told him harshly. He explained about the ill-fated invasion force and their abortive attempts at securing a groundside front.

"I didn't think you were from around here," Rand said, somewhat relieved. "Admiral Hunter, huh?" It was as if Scott had mentioned George Washington.

"Ancient history, I suppose."

Rand shrugged. "I've never heard of Reflex Point either. 'Course, I don't mix much when I don't have to. As far as I know, the Invid HQ is north of here—*way* north." Fascinated, he watched as Scott, now on his knees, collapsed and stepped out of the two-wheeled backpack, returning the mecha to Cyclone configuration. "You really going to try and find Reflex?"

"That's what I'm here for," said Scott, doffing the helmet. As he pulled it over his head, the chin strap caught the holo-locket's chain and took it along. The heart fell and opened, replaying its brief message to Scott and his stunned companion.

"... *I'm looking forward to living the rest of my life with you. I can't wait till this conflict is all behind us. Till we meet again, my love* ..."

Wordlessly, Scott stooped to retrieve the heart.
"Hey, that's great!" said Rand. "Is that your girl?"
"Uh ... my girl," Scott stammered. He straightened up, clutching the heart against his pectoral armor, and turned his back to Rand.

CHAPTER
THREE

Dolza's annihilation bolts had devastated the South American coastal cities and turned much of the vast interior forest into wasteland. Ironically enough, however, repopulation of the area was largely the result of the hundreds of Zentraedi warships that crashed there after the firing of the Grand Cannon. Indeed, even after Khyron's efforts to stage a full-scale rebellion had failed, the region was still largely under Zentraedi domination (the T'sentrati Control Zone, as it was known to the indigenous peoples), up until the Malcontent uprisings of 2013–15 and the subsequent events headed up by Captain Maxmillian Sterling of the Robotech Defense Force. But contrary to popular belief, Brazilas did not become the lawless frontier Scott Bernard traversed until much later, specifically, the two-year period between the fall of Chairman Moran's Council and the Invid invasion. In fact the region had seen extensive changes during the Second Robotech War and surely would have risen to the fore had it not been for the disastrous end to that fifteen-year epoch.

"Southlands," *History of the Third Robotech War,*
Vol. XXII

COUNTLESS PEOPLE FOUND THEMSELVES HOME-less after the Invid's preemptive strike against Earth; the waste was awash with wanderers, thieves, and madmen. And, of course, children: lost, uprooted, orphaned. They fared worse than the other groups, usually falling prey to illness, starvation, and marauding gangs. Occasionally, one would stumble upon groups of them in devastated cities or natural shelters—caves, patches of forest, oases—forty or fifty strong, banded together like some feral family; and God help the one who tried to disturb their new order!...But this was the exception rather than the rule. The great majority of them had to make their own way and fend for themselves, attach themselves—more often, *enslave* themselves—to whomever or whatever could provide them with some semblance of protection, the chance for a better tomorrow.

Laako City, largest settlement in the southern wastes, saw its fair share of these nameless drifters, and Ken was usually the one who welcomed them with open arms. He was a tall, gangly streetwise eighteen-year-old with a reputation for dirty tricks, mean-spirited by nature but a charmer when he needed to be. His long hair was a pewter color, save for the crimson forelock that was his trademark.

His most recent conquest was a young girl named Annie, who claimed to be fifteen. But Ken had grown bored with her; besides, he had his eye fixed on a pretty little dark-haired urchin who had just arrived in Laako, and the time had come to kiss Annie off.

The trouble was that Annie didn't want to go.

"Don't leave me like this!" she was pleading with him just now, alligator tears coursing down moon-face cheeks.

"Hey," he told her soothingly, disengaging himself from her hold on his arm. "You knew from the start you'd have to leave someday."

This was and was not true: Laako did maintain a policy of limiting the time outsiders were allowed to spend in the city, but well-connected Ken could easily have steered his way around the regs. If he had been so inclined.

The two of them were standing at the causeway entrance to the city in the lake, the tall albeit ruined towers of the Laako's twin islands visible in the background. Sundry trucks and tractors on their way to the causeway checkpoint were motoring by, kicking up dust and decibels alike.

"*Please*, Ken!" Annie tried, emphatically this time, launching herself at him, hoping to pinion his arms with her small hands. It was push and pull for a moment— Ken saying, "Annie!... Cut it out!... Stop it!" to Annie's "I can't!... I won't!... I can't!—" but ultimately he put a violent end to it, bringing his arms up with such force that Annie was thrown to the ground.

Which was easy enough for him to do. She was a good foot shorter than Ken, with a large mouth, long, straight, carrot-colored hair, and what some might have termed a cherublike cuteness about her. Her single outfit consisted of an olive-drab double-breasted military jumpsuit she had picked up along the trail, set off by a pink frameless rucksack and a maroon visored cap emblazoned with the letters *E.T.*, a piece of twentieth-century nostalgia that dated back to a popular science-fantasy film. It was difficult to tell—as it was with many of the lost—whether Annie was searching for a friend, a father, or a lover. And it was doubtful that she could have answered the question either.

"I *told* you to cut it out," Ken started to say, but the sight of her kneeling in the dirt crying her eyes out managed to touch what meager tenderness he still possessed. "Don't you see I have no choice?" he continued apologetically, walking over to her and placing his hand on her heaving shoulder. "This whole thing is just as hard for me as it is for you, Annie. Please try and understand."

She kept her face buried in her hands, sobbing while he spoke.

"Nobody who comes from the outside can stay for more than a little while, remember? And if I left here, I wouldn't be allowed to return..."

Suddenly the tears were gone and she was looking up at him with a devious grin on her face. "Then run away with me, Ken! We'll start our *own* family, our own *town*!" She was up on her feet now, tugging on his arm, but Ken didn't budge.

"Quit giving me a hard time," he told her harshly, angry at himself for being taken in by her saltwater act. "I'm not going anywhere—*you* are!"

Annie's face contorted through sorrow to rage. She cursed him, using everything her vocabulary had to offer. But in return he proffered a knowing smile that undermined her anger. "You're heartless," she seethed, collapsing to the ground once more. "Heartless."

Rand had led Scott to the site of the downed transport; the Mars Division commander held little hope that anyone had survived the crash but thought there might be an Armored Alpha Veritech still aboard. He was thankful for the Cyclone, but with perhaps thousands of miles separating him from the Invid Reflex Point, the journey would be a long one indeed.

Fearing a visit from Invid reinforcements—Shock Troopers this time—the two riders didn't remain long at the wreck. There were neither survivors nor Veritechs, but Scott was at least able to procure additional Scorpions for the battle armor launchers, several canisters of Protoculture fuel, and a sensor-studded helmet for Rand. Thus far the redheaded rebel had demonstrated no inclination to form even a temporary partnership, but Scott hoped that the helmet and battle armor would entice him somewhat. Scott would have been the first to admit his sense of helplessness; he was a stranger to this world and its ways. And if the unthinkable had occurred—if he alone had survived the atmospheric plunge—he was going to need all the help he could get.

Rand wasn't sure what to make of the offworlder. He was a good man to have on one's side in a fight and no doubt a capable enough officer in his own element, but he was a fish out of water on Earth, and a relic besides

—a throwback to a time when humankind functioned hopefully and collectively. In any case, Rand was a lone rider, and he meant to keep it that way. You joined up with someone, and suddenly there were compromises that had to be made, plans and decisions a single Forager wasn't caught up in.

Rand lived for the open road, and he was grateful that the offworlder hadn't lingered too long at the crash site, glad to have it behind him now. The two had ridden as far as the hills together, then Rand had waved Scott off and lit out on his own, the Cyclone throbbing beneath him. He was enchanted with the mecha, but there were a few other priorities that needed tending to: food, for starters. The tasteless stuff Scott had liberated from the wreck might be all right for spacemen, but it wasn't likely to catch on among down-to-earth Foragers.

Once again he had decided to pass on Laako City; it would be easy enough to get something to eat there, but the results probably wouldn't justify the paranoid garbage he would have to put up with. Rand had never visited Laako, but what he had heard from other Foragers was enough to give him second thoughts about the place.

Even so, he was headed in the general direction of the island city, putting the Cyclone through the paces on the twisting mountain road that connected the wastes with the grasslands and lakes of the central plateaus. The only such road, it was usually heavily trafficked and dangerous in spots—little more than a narrow ledge with deep ruts and steep drop-offs. But most of that was still ahead of him, and he was cruising along, oblivious to the fact that Scott was not far behind. Then Rand heard the roar of the second Cyclone and looked over his right shoulder, surprised to find the offworlder scrambling along the embankment above the roadway. Scott gave a nod and piloted the cycle through a clean jump that brought him alongside Rand.

"What's the problem?" Rand shouted, raising his goggles. "You got nowhere to go, or what?" He saw Scott smile beneath the helmet's wraparound chin guard.

"I want to head up toward that city you mentioned," Scott called back, maintaining his speed. "We might be able to get some information."

"What's this *we* stuff, spaceman?" Rand barked. "I go my own way."

Scott smiled again. "Come on, I'll show you how to convert to Battle Armor mode. Or maybe you're too frightened of the Invid, huh?"

"Hey, pal, *you* go ahead and wage your one-man war. This Cyclone's fine as is," Rand snapped. "See you around," he added, giving a twist to the throttle and pulling out ahead of Scott.

In a moment Scott came up alongside again.

"Make up your mind—you headed to the city or not?"

Scott made a gesture of nonchalance. "I'm just headed where I'm headed, that's all."

"Well, get off my tail!" Rand shouted, lowering his goggles. He popped the front wheel and accelerated out front.

Scott did the same, and the two of them toyed with each other for several minutes, alternating the lead. By now they had entered the shoulderless downhill portion of the highway, and Rand was nursing some misgivings about playing chicken with a dude who was decked out in armor. Nevertheless, he stuck by the offworlder, racing him into a wide turn where the roadway disappeared around the shoulder of the mountain. Neither of them saw the convoy of trucks headed for the pass until it was almost too late. The driver of the lead vehicle—an open-cabbed eight-wheeler—leaned on his horn and locked up the brakes, throwing the transport into zigzags. The Cyclones, meanwhile, were also locked up, sliding sideways down the narrow road. Rand, on the inside, saw a collapsed portion of an earthen wall and went for it, ramping his bike up to the high ground. Scott, however, kept to the road, dangerously close to the drop-off now, and brought the Cyclone to a halt a meter from the truck's front grille.

The driver, a long-haired rube wearing a tall brimmed hat, waved his fist in the air. "Ya rogue—somebody coulda got killed!"

"Sorry about that," Scott told him offhandedly. "Look, we need some information—"

"Wait a minute!" the driver cut Scott off, eyeing him up and down. "You're a soldier! What are you doing out here?"

Scott revealed just enough to satisfy the driver's curiosity. "I'm looking for others who may have bailed out. Have you come across anyone?" Scott saw the man give a start, then avert his gaze.

"Nope. No one . . . But lemme give you a free piece of advice," the driver answered him, throwing the truck into forward gear. "You're gonna wish you never came back!"

Scott legged the Cyclone off to one side, calling out for an explanation as the truck roared off. The other drivers in the convoy regarded Scott warily from the cabs of their trucks as they lumbered by, but no one said a word until a young boy in the back of the final one yelled out: "Hey, mister, don't tell anyone who you are or you'll be in deep trouble!"

Scott thought he would hear more, but the truck's headbanded elder put a hand over the boy's mouth. "Don't talk to that man," he threatened the kid.

Rand watched the convoy disappear around the bend and saw Scott's gesture of puzzlement. "You coming or not?" the offworlder asked him suddenly. Rand thought about it for a moment while Scott took off down the road. All his instincts told him to follow the trucks, but ultimately he coasted down the incline and set out to catch up with Scott; after all, *somebody* had to keep the guy from sticking his nose where it didn't belong.

In the trees at the edge of the roadway, the red optic scanner of an Invid Scout rotated slightly to track the rider's swift departure....

"Ken, *please* come with me!" Annie was shouting. "I'll be good for you, I promise! I love you! You promised you'd stay with me!"

He was dragging her down the road now, his hands underneath her arms. They were a good half mile from the causeway checkpoints already, and Annie was still causing a scene. Finally he dropped her on her butt.

"Whaddaya want from me—you want me to leave my family and friends?"

She looked up at him and said, "Yes."

Ken bent down eye to eye with her. "Look, I know it seems bad right now, but you'll find somebody to take care of you."

"Don't worry about me!" she yelled in his face as she got up. "I can find my own way around. Men are a dime a dozen for someone like me." Then suddenly she was all over him again: "*Please*, Ken!"

Ken shook her off, sending her down to the ground on her knees. Fed up, he began to walk back to the checkpoint. Ten steps away, however, he turned at the sound of approaching vehicles. Scott and Rand were just coming around a bend in the tree-lined road. They halted their Cyclones where Annie sat crying. Ken took one look at the cycles and saw a sweet deal in the making. He went over to them with a gleam in his eye.

Closest to Annie, Rand was asking, "What's the matter, kid, are you hurt?"

She looked up, surprised, and told him in no uncertain terms that *she wasn't a kid.* "So, beat it!"

Ken ambled up and gestured appreciatively at Scott's mecha. "Nice wheels, rogue." Ken smiled. "Where'd you forage 'em?"

"I'm Commander Bernard of Mars Division," Scott said when he had raised the helmet faceshield. "I'm looking for other survivors of my unit."

Ken glanced over at Rand and stepped back. "You're for real, then—soldiers, I mean."

"Have you seen any of the others?"

"Come with me," Ken said after a moment, already setting off for the causeway.

Scott was suddenly full of hope. "They're here?"

"And you can come, too, Annie," Ken added without turning around.

Annie's eyes opened wide. "I take back what I said." She hurried to catch up with him and attached herself to his arm lovingly.

Rand and Scott exchanged looks and brought the Cyclones back to life. "What's the chance of landing some belly timber?" Rand wanted to know. "We've got trade goods."

"Follow me," Ken told him.

Annie beamed. "You've made me so happy, Ken." She went up on tiptoe to kiss him on the mouth.

Ken whisked them through the checkpoint and escorted them along the causeway that led to the main island. It was a picturesque spot for a city, Rand had to admit: a crystal-blue lake surrounded by forested hills. But there was ample evidence of the war's hold over the place—the scorched and rusted hulks of Zentraedi battlecruisers, downed Adventurers, Falcons, and Bioroids.

He noticed that there was a second island, accessible only from the main one, and that it, too, was host to a densely packed cluster of tall, mostly ruined buildings, rubble, and debris heaped up in the streets. Up close the city was somewhat less than inspiring, literally a shell of its former self, but so far they hadn't been searched, hassled, or otherwise bad-vibed, and Rand was beginning to wonder where all those rumors had come from.

"These are Robotech soldiers!" Ken announced to the sullen-faced people huddled inside the buildings, postapocalypse cave dwellers in high-rise cliffs of slagged steel and fractured concrete. "They were with the forces who have returned to Earth to rid us of the Invid." No one moved, no one returned a word. There was only the slight howling of the wind and the steady throb of the Cyclones' engines. "They're looking for lost members of the assault group. I'm going to take them over to the other island."

Ken turned a wan smile to Scott and Rand. "As you can see, folks around here aren't used to strangers," he said by way of apology. "They're always a bit suspicious at first, but don't worry about it. They'll soon get used to you."

Scott, Rand, and Annie followed Ken's lead to the causeway linking the main island with its twin.

"There it is." Ken pointed. "If any of your comrades have come through here, they'll have been taken over to the other island."

"Thanks a lot for your help, Ken," Scott said.

Ken disengaged his hand from Annie's two-fisted lock on it. "Why don't you show them over the causeway while I go talk to the Elders about your staying here?"

Annie called out to him as he was walking away.

"Yes?" he said impatiently, not bothering to turn around.

"Bye-bye, sweet thing!"

"And don't forget that food!" Rand thought to add.

Annie made an elaborate gesture, then laughed. "Now, if you gentlemen will just follow me . . ."

Rand chuckled and patted the rear seat of the Cyclone. "Hop on," he told her. "It'll be fun."

CHAPTER
FOUR

The Invid Regis ruled her empire from Reflex Point (located in what was once the United States of America, specifically the Indiana-Ohio frontier); but there was scarcely a region without one or two large hives (except the poles and vast uninhabited tracts in Asia and Africa). In this way her Scouts were always about, with Enforcers (a.k.a. Shock Troopers) not far behind. Brazilas was no different from other northern regions in that it was effectively an occupied zone. Like Vichy France of the Second World War, each town had its sympathizers and resistance fighters; but the former far outnumbered the latter, and it was not uncommon to encounter gruesome and ghastly acts of betrayal and butchery undertaken in the name of self-survival.

Bloom Nesterfig, *Social Organization of the Invid*

As RAND HIMSELF WOULD LATER WRITE:

"There was something about Ken's telling Annie to lead us across the causeway that hit me like a cold wind, but for some reason I just turned my back to it. Scott's innocent enthusiasm had something to do with this. Psyched about seeing some of his friends, he was off in a flash, the Cyclone's rear end chirping a quick good-bye to me and the kid. So I told her to climb on and followed Scott's carefree course, Annie laughing and hanging on for dear life while I goosed the mecha into a long goldcard wheelie.

"The bridge was a simple affair, a flat span no more than fifteen feet wide and a quarter mile long, its plastar surface every bit as holed and bellied as the rest of Laako's streets. The causeway seemed to bisect the island's stand of colorless truncated towers, which rose before us like some ruined vision of the future, an emerald without its shine. Beyond it, a ridge of green hills and a soft-looking autumn sky.

"Scott was a block or two ahead of me when we hit the island, and talk about your low-rent downtown... the place looked as though it had seen some intense fighting with conventional weapons as well as the usual Robo upgrades. Scott had slowed his cycle to a crawl and was using the mecha's externals to broadcast our arrival.

"'This is Commander Bernard of the Twenty-first Armored Tactical Assault Squadron,' his voice rang out. 'I'm looking for any Mars Division survivors. If you can hear my voice, please respond...Is anybody there? I just want to talk!'

"Annie and I looked around but didn't see anyone moving. I would have been happy to see some more of those sunken-eyed citizens we had seen on the other side, but suddenly even those shadowy cliff dwellers were in short supply. Up ahead, Scott was stopped near a pile of trashed mecha, a perverse war memorial complete with Veritechs, Battlepods, Hovertanks, and Bioroids, arms, legs, and cannon muzzles fused together in a kind of death-affirming sculpture. I came up behind him and toed the Cyclone into neutral. We were on a small rise above the causeway, Scott off to my left, staring at the junk heap with a kind of morbid fascination.

"Then we saw the Cyclones.

"And the bodies.

"You couldn't ride the wastes in those days and be a stranger to death, and like everyone I had seen my fair share of Human remains, but there were fresh kills in the heap, and it was obvious what had happened.

"'This isn't any junk pile!' I heard Scott say. 'It's a goddamn graveyard!'

"Annie gave a start and hugged herself to my back. 'What's it mean?' she cried, panic already in her voice.

"Scott glanced over at us, his face all twisted up. 'It means I smell a rat and it's got your boyfriend's face!'

"All at once we heard a deep whirring noise accompanied by sounds of mechanical disengagement. I looked back toward the causeway in time to see it give a shudder, then begin a slow retraction toward the main island. But I was more puzzled than alarmed. I'd already seen Scott leap that mecha of his twice the distance to the island, so our being able to get off this one alive only meant that I was going to be learning the secrets of Cyclone reconfiguration in spite of myself. Moreover, I couldn't figure why Ken needed to resort to such elaborate plans to rid Laako of intruders.

"I think Scott must have been way ahead of me on this one, because he didn't seem at all surprised when two Invid suddenly surfaced in the lake. Annie's pounding me on the back, shouting, 'We gotta get outta here!' and Scott is just sitting silently on the Cyclone taking in the situation like he's got all the time in the world. I'll always remember the look on his face at that moment— and I would have reason to recall it often during the following months. I thought to myself: *The eye of the storm.*

"Two more Invid were now heading our way from up the street, looming over us, pincers gleaming like knives caught in the light, the ground shaking from their footfalls. These weren't Scouts but Shock Troopers, the larger, meaner version whose shoulder-mounted organic-looking cannons gave them a wide-eyed amphibious look. The lake creatures had submerged, only to reappear behind us, rising up through the plastar streets and putting a radical end to thoughts of escape. In a moment the four were joined by a fifth, who had also taken the subterranean route.

"I felt compelled to point out that we were surrounded, and Scott said, 'Take off!' Which I was all for. I spun the cycle around my left foot and was gone, Scott not two lengths behind me, his Cyclone launched from the street by an overhead pincer slam that nearly flattened him. Later, Annie apologized for the fingernail prints she left in my upper arms, but at that moment I was feeling no pain.

"I had what I thought was the presence of mind to head for the narrower streets, but the Troopers were determined to have us for lunch; their leader, airborne now, simply used its shoulders to power a wider upper-story path between the buildings.

"'How'd they find us!' Annie was yelling into my left ear.

"'Your boyfriend, Ken,' I told her. 'He delivered us right into their claws.' But she didn't want to hear it. Who—*Ken*?

"'He'd never do anything like that—*never!*'

"It wasn't really a good time for an argument, though. The Troopers were sticking to us like magnets, firing off bursts of plasma fire. The fact that I had seen what those annihilation discs could do to a Human body was probably responsible for the chancy moves I made on the Cyclone. But the memory of those liquid remains paid off, because I got us through the first stretch unscathed. Then, after we had taken them around one block, down an alleyway, and through half a dozen more right angles, Scott told me to get the kid out of there; he was going Battle Armor to lure them away. Scott was nothing if not noble. But I couldn't resist getting another look at that reconfiguration act, and caught some flack for it.

"'What're you *looking* at?' Scott berated me over the externals. 'Get moving!'

"Annie seconded this with a couple of cleanly placed kidney shots. So Scott and I parted company at a T intersection, and the next thing I heard was a massive exchange of cannonfire and a series of crippling explosions. But the Invid had done their part in sticking to Scott's tail, and Annie and I were in the clear for the moment.

"I pulled the bike over and told her to hop off. There was no way I was going to let Scott take all the heat; I just had to get my Cyclone to reconfigure, battle armor or not. Trouble was, the damn thing wouldn't respond. I thumbed the switch above the starter button, but nothing happened, so I started flipping switches left and right, cursing the thing for being so obstinate. Annie, the little darling, stood by me, hands behind her head, taunting me and telling me in no uncertain terms to hurry the hell up. Of course, I have since learned that that is precisely what you *don't* do with a piece of mecha, but what did this basically backwoods loner know about mecha then? I just kept jiggling this, pounding that, turning the other, and all of a sudden I found myself flat on my back in the seat, the Cyclone grotesquely reconfigured, with both wheels behind it now, its nose kissing the street.

"Annie was kind enough not to laugh in my face; she turned aside first. And I did something brilliant—like leap off the cycle and try to place kick it into the lake—which only resulted in an injury to my foot to match the one already sustained by my pride.

"But now Annie was shouting and pointing up at something. Scott, in full battle armor, had taken to the buttressed top of a building a few blocks away. One minute he was standing there like some sort of rooftop Robostatue, and the next he was playing dodge-the-plasma-Frisbees. I saw him drop into that annihilation disc storm and execute one of those Bernard bounces that carried him out of sight, just short of the explosions that turned the building into a chimney, flames roaring up from its blasted roof, black parabolas of slagged stuff in the sky.

"Meanwhile, I had worked through my frustration and managed to get the mecha back into Cycle mode. Annie still wanted to know why the thing wouldn't change. I started to explain about the armor and 'thinking cap,' and the next thing I knew she was running off toward the causeway.

"'I'm gonna go and find Ken and get him to tell me once and for all why he went and sold us out to the Invid!' she yelled after I tried to get her to stop. ''F you don't like it—*tough*!'

"I had to admit that I was thinking along those very same lines, but Annie's timing left a lot to be desired. And since I didn't relish the thought of finding that pink backpack of hers dangling from a bloody pincer, I threw the Cyclone into gear and went after her. I reached out, and she swatted my hand away, telling me to get lost. Angry now, I decided I would just scoop her up in my left arm and put an end to the foolishness, but I misjudged both my course and her weight. No sooner did my arm go around her waist than I was pulled from the mecha. Worse still, we were right alongside an open freight elevator; and down we went, eight feet or more, would-be opponents wrapped in each other's arms.

"I blacked out for a moment; perhaps we both did. But Annie came around first and laid into me as though I had just tried to maul her. I came to with her shouting: 'Get off of me, you monster! You dirty Forager sleaze! You're all alike!' She heaved me off her and scrambled up out of the shaft with a nimbleness and speed that surprised me. By the time I poked my head out, she was nowhere in sight. But I heard her rummaging around in a nearby pile of mecha scrap, still cursing men in general, me in particular. When I saw her come up with an old-fashioned automatic rifle, I started having second thoughts about showing myself. Fortunately, she was only interested in emptying the thing's clip against the already devastated facade of a building across the street. Then she tossed the depleted thing aside and dove back down into the scrap heap. Meanwhile, I was wondering what had become of Scott and whether the Invid would home in on Annie's gunfire. When I looked over at her again, she was wrestling an antitank weapon up onto her shoulder.

"'Watch where you point that thing!' I started to warn her. 'It might be—'

"And it was.

"The small missile nearly put a center part in my hair, then changed trajectory and detonated against the side of the building.

"A little to the right and she would have connected with the Invid who was just stepping around that same corner.

"I ran for the overturned Cyclone, hopped on, and darted over to pick up Annie, who now had control of the weapon. She located another missile and launched it against the approaching Shock Trooper. I backed her up with Scorpions from the front-end launch tubes of the Cyclone, but neither of us managed to connect with a soft spot in the thing's shell, and it kept up its menacing advance. Annie screamed and made a run for it, not a second before the creature's right claw came down at her; the tip of its bladelike pincer swept the pack from her back and ripped open the jumpsuit neck to waist but left her otherwise untouched. But the nearness of the blow paralyzed her; I saw her reach back, finger the tear, and collapse to her knees.

"Meanwhile, I had problems of my own: The Invid had turned its attention to me and fired off several discs, one of which blew the Cyclone out from under me and threw me a good fifteen feet from the blast. My back was to its advance now, but one look at Annie's shocked face told me everything I needed to know.

"'Heeelp!' she was screaming. *'Anyone!'*

"But there was something else in my line of sight as well: a glint across the lake, sunshine on gleaming metal. And even as my head was going down to the street in a gesture of surrender and ultimate indifference—some part of my warped mind wondering what that giant cloven foot or pincer was going to feel like—I knew Annie's call had been heard.

"A figure in red Cyclone battle armor launched itself across the lake and came down at the end of the street, hopping in for a rescue, dodging one, two, then three explosive blasts from the Invid Shock Trooper. I saw the soldier return fire from the rifle/cannon portion of the armor's right arm and heard the Invid take a direct hit and come apart.

"The soldier put down behind me as I rolled over, Annie *ooh*ing and *ahh*ing nearby, just in time to see Scott appear at the other end of the street with three Invid on his tail. He dropped one for the crowd and took off out of sight, the other two closing on him. I got up, hand shielding my eyes, and tried to follow the fight. Overhead now, Scott blasted a second Invid, then swooped in low and ass-backward to finish off the last. I saw him sight in on the Trooper, then loose the shot. It tore into one of the Invid's hemispheric cranial protrusions, loosing fire and smoke from the hole.

"Scott was thrown backward by the missile's kick and landed on his butt not ten feet in front of us—Annie, me, and the mysterious red Cycloner. The Invid came in on residuals, mimicking Scott's undignified approach with one of its own, and immediately fell face forward to the street, a sickly green fluid spewing from its wound, its outstretched pincer trapping and nearly mincing poor Annie. Scott had explained that the fluid was a kind of nutrient derived from the Flowers of Life, but I had yet to see exactly what it was that the stuff was keeping alive! Scott, his faceshield raised, turned to thank the red who had come to our aid. But it was obvious he had seen something I hadn't, because he stopped in midsentence, as though questioning what he was seeing.

"And Red bounded off without a word.

"At the same time, Annie was crying for help, and Scott went over to her, lifting the pincer enough to allow the pale and shaken kid to crawl free. What a picture she made, kneeling there in the dirt, tears cascading down her face, her torn jumpsuit hanging off her shoulders.

"'I'm so sorry,' she wailed. 'This is all my fault.'

"Scott didn't say anything; he simply walked over to the fallen Invid and regarded it—analytically, I thought, as though he had seen those things bleed before.

"I was sitting on the engine cover of my overturned Cyclone feeling twenty years older and wondering what had happened to solo riding.

"'We did what we could,' I told Scott. 'But it just wasn't enough.'

"Annie said, 'Now what are we going to do, Rand?'

"And Scott and I exchanged looks, remembering Ken and the other island . . .''

"We found Annie's knapsack, and I did what I could to sew up the tear in her jumpsuit. The causeway had been reextended to complete the span between the islands; Scott figured that Ken and the others had heard the explosions and realized they were going to have to deal with us one way or another. This was pretty much the case. Ken said, 'I'm glad you made it,' when he saw us cycle in. But Annie wasn't buying it; she leaped off the rear seat, even before I had brought the Cyclone to a halt, and whacked Ken across the face forcefully enough to spin him around. He gave us a brief over-the-shoulder look and decided he had better take it or he would have us coming down on him as well.

"He asked Annie to forgive him, and frankly, I was surprised by the sincerity he managed to dredge up. 'I only did it to save the others,' he explained. 'If we stood up to the Invid, all the people in Laako would suffer for it. The way things are, we get by all right.'

"Fire in his eyes, Scott dismounted, took off his helmet, and walked over to Ken. 'So you feed potential troublemakers to the Invid to save your own skins,' he growled.

"I'm not sure what would have happened next if a crowd of Laako's citizenry hadn't appeared.

"'You got that right, soldier!' their leader told Scott.

"They were only a dozen strong, men, women, and children, and they were unarmed; but there was an attitude of defiance about them that rattled us. The rest of the audience was glaring down at us from their cells in those shells of buildings.

"'You've got to leave here!' the man continued. 'I'm sorry, but we don't want any soldiers in this town. So get out—now!'

"I had to hand it to the guy: He wasn't especially large or well built, and his glasses and workman's blues gave him a kind of paternal look; but here he was standing up to an offworlder in Cyclone battle armor. I thought Scott would take the poor man apart; instead, I heard him laugh.

"'Well, was it something we said?' Scott asked.

"'There is nothing funny about the situation, young man,' the man responded angrily. 'I am in deadly earnest. Nobody here even wanted your Robotech Expeditionary Mission to begin with, and if it wasn't for you soldiers, this planet would still be living in peace! Now, get out! Save your rescues for somewhere else!'

"I winced at hearing this, knowing the man had gone

too far. Scott stepped into the guy's face, shouting back: 'Why you. . . . Don't you realize that without any kind of resistance, you've got no hope?!'

"'We know,' Ken chimed in from behind Scott. 'But we still want you to leave.'

"'Terrific,' Scott snarled. 'You're going to sit back and relax and let the Invid rule over you and the entire planet—'

"'Fighting the Invid will aggravate the whole situation!' the crowd leader interrupted. 'All we want is a peaceful life. What difference does it make who's at the top—some corrupt Council or the Invid? There's no such thing as freedom!'

"The man must have caught a whiff of his own words, because all of a sudden he was soft-spoken and rational. 'Look, anybody who hasn't seen it our way has already left. So will you please go?'

"I had heard the same speech so often that I hardly paid any attention to it, but you just didn't go throwing the reality of the situation into the face of a guy who had come halfway across the galaxy to fight your battles for you. Before I could open my mouth, Scott had grabbed the guy by the shirtfront and was ready to split his head open.

"I told Scott to leave him alone. After all, in their own way they were right: They had peaceful lives, even without the so-called freedoms that were so important thirty years ago. Besides, nothing Scott or I could say or do was going to change the way they felt.

"'Look around you,' I told Scott.

"He did, and the truth of it seemed to sink in some. He shoved the man aside and spat in the street. 'I don't believe what I'm witnessing here,' he rebuked the crowd. 'You people make me sick! You think I'm the only one fighting the Invid? Well, there are plenty of others. People who aren't ready to roll over and play dead, understand?'

"The crowd looked at him pityingly. He donned his helmet, mounted the Cyclone, and took off without a word to any of us.

"I felt that I had to back Scott up and made some kind of silly speech about selling out strangers, but it all fell on deaf ears. Except Annie's.

"'That goes for me, too,' she told the crowd. 'I wouldn't want to live in this rotten town anyway.' With that, she threw herself onto the cycle's rear seat and told me to 'let 'er rip.'

"Annie hugged herself to me for all it was worth, and I could almost feel her tears through my shirt. But when I asked if she was okay, she said she would make it all right. I was certain she had known worse moments in her life. . . .

"When we caught up with Scott, I asked about his plans.

"'Somehow or other I've got to find Reflex Point,' he yelled without bothering to look over at me.

"He had mentioned this when we first met and once or twice since but had never explained its meaning. 'You keep talking about this place as if it's the most important thing in the world.'

"'It is,' Scott threw back sternly, and accelerated out front.

"There was something about his attitude that put me off, or maybe I was just hoping for an argument that would split us up and return me to my solo riding. I said, 'You know what your problem is? You don't know how to communicate with people! Now that you've had a taste of the old homeworld, don't you think you'd be a lot happier back in space with your girlfriend?'

"His silence told me I'd gotten to him.

"'Lay off,' he snapped back, accelerating again. 'Marlene's dead.'

"It literally stopped me cold in my tracks.

"'He never told you?' Annie said as we watched Scott disappear over a rise up ahead.

"'Not one word about it,' I mumbled. It explained a lot about Scott's behavior, his obsession with waging this one-man war of his. . . .

"'I know how he feels,' Annie was saying. 'Being the woman so many men dream of, and yet so unlucky in love, has made me very sensitive to this sort of thing.'

"I didn't know whether she was trying to make me laugh or what, but her comment succeeded in lightening my spirits. Then she slammed me on the back: 'Hey, come on! We're gonna lose Scott if we don't get a move on!'

"I asked her if she was sure about leaving Ken behind, and she made a face.

"'Uh-huh. I have a feeling my next lover's going to be my last. Now, let's get moving, Rand!'

"She pounded her tiny fists against my back again, and we were gone."

FIVE

> *Mom was, as they used to say at the turn of the century, one tough broad. She was the most respected member of the Blue Angels, and even after her falling out with Romy and her flight from Cavern City, her name was adopted by only those riders who shot for the narrows, and scrawled on many a wall.*
>
> Maria Bartley-Rand, *Flower of Life: Journey Beyond Protoculture*

IT WASN'T MUCH OF A TOWN—STRICTLY MAIN-STREET frontier, run-down and dirty—and it wasn't much of a bar, but at least the place offered cold beer (even if it was locally brewed and bitter-tasting), shade, and a singer backed by a decent pickup band.

> After all of the battles are over
> After all of the fighting is done
> Will you be the one
> To find yourself alone with your heart
> Looking for the answer?

Rook Bartley lifted her glass and toasted the singer. The song was soft and downbeat, just what she needed to ease herself into the blues, trip through memories she couldn't do anything about.

Rook took a look around the place over the rim of her mug. It was dimly lit and poorly ventilated but surprisingly clean and tidy for a joint in the wastes. There was the usual assortment of types, Foragers mostly, keeping to themselves in the corners, nursing drinks and private thoughts. A couple or two wrapped around each other on the cleared space that passed for a dance floor. And several bad boys on the upper tier, boots up on the table, midnight shades. Rook judged they were locals from the way they were scanning the room for action, your basic rough trade feeling safe on the barren piece of turf they had secured for themselves. Rook returned to her drink, unimpressed.

She was a petite and shapely eighteen-year-old with a mane of strawberry-blond hair and a face that more than one man had fallen in love with. She was wearing a red and white short-sleeved bodysuit that hugged her in all the right places. It was set off by forearm sheaths, a blue utility belt, and boots, an outfit styled to match the mecha she rode, a red Cyclone she had liberated from an armory just after her split from the Blue Angels, the assault by the Snakes. . . .

When it feels like tomorrow will never come
When it seems like the night will not end
Can you pretend
That you're really not alone?
You're out here on your own
(Lonely soldier boy)
You're out here on your own
(Lonely soldier boy)

Rook settled back in her chair to study the group's lead singer, a rocker well known in the wastes who called herself Yellow Dancer. The song had taken an unanticipated leap to four-four, guitar and keyboards wailing, and Yellow was off to one side of the low stage, clapping in time and allowing the band their moment in the spots. She was tall and rather broad-shouldered, Rook thought, but attractive in a way that appealed to men and women both. Her hair was long but shagged, tinted slightly lavender and held by a green leather band that chevroned in the center of her forehead. Yellow's stage clothes were not at all elaborate—pumps, tight-fitting slacks, and a strapless top trimmed in purple—but were well suited to her tall frame and flattering to her figure.

Yellow stepped back to the mike to acknowledge the applause. She was modest and smiling until one of the bad boys decided to change the tempo somewhat.

"Hey, baby face!" he called out, getting up from the table and approaching the stage. "Me and my friends don't like your music. It stinks, y' hear?"

Rook had expected as much. It was the one with the pointed chin and wraparound sunglasses, the apparent gang leader. He was wearing tight jeans tucked into suede shin boots and a short-sleeve shirt left unbuttoned.

"It's garbage, it ain't music," he insulted the singer.

Rook wondered how Yellow would handle it; the pickup band were locals, as was most of the room. No one was exactly rising to her defense, but neither was she showing signs of concern.

"Well, why don't you just give these people a sample of what *you* consider music?" she taunted back.

Some of the crowd found the comeback amusing, which only managed to put Yellow's critic on the spot. Rather than risk making a fool of himself, he decided to teach her a quick lesson and stepped forward swinging a lightning right.

"I'll give 'em a sample," he said at the same time.

But Yellow was even faster; still maintaining her place, she ducked to the left, leaving vacuum in her wake. The rogue's arm sailed clean through nothingness, wrapping itself around the mike stand, and threw him completely off balance. The crowd howled, and Yellow smiled. But in that instant, her assailant recollected himself, turned, and caught her across the face with an open-hand left.

Yellow's head snapped back, but not for long. She countered with a right, open-hand also but hooked a bit to bring her nails into play. The man took the blow full force to his temple and cheek; his glasses were knocked askew, and blood had been drawn.

"Now we're even," she said to the leader, whose back was still turned to her. But she now had the rest of the gang to answer to as well; they had left their tables and were approaching her threateningly. "How about calling it quits, fellahs?" she told them. "Tag-team wrestling isn't scheduled until Saturday night, and we wouldn't want to mess up the program, would we?"

Rook had to laugh; either she knew what she was doing or she was one of those who got her kicks face-down. Rook had reason to believe it was the former, however. Yellow was set like an upsprung trap, her legs slightly bent, her fists clawed. At the same time, she was keeping an eye on the one she had already wounded and was more than ready for him when he pounced.

"You little witch!" the man snarled. "I'll kill you!"

He moved in and swung a roundhouse left with little of the lightning that had characterized his first swing and none of the ambivalence of the second. But once again, Yellow was left untouched, and the momentum carried the man off the stage, practically into the arms of his henchmen.

"I've enjoyed our little dancing lesson," Yellow joked, backing away somewhat. "But if it's all the same to you, this place is paying me to *sing*." Her eyes darted right and left, plotting an escape if needed. "Of course, we can pick up where we left off after the show—you could sure use some work on your fox-trot, you know—and if you're all nice boys, I'll teach you to rumba. . . ."

The gang was closing in on her, and Rook was beginning to rethink her earlier evaluation of Yellow Dancer. Whatever happened now, she had some of it coming. Meanwhile the club owner had appeared on the stage to intercede. But Rook had to laugh again, grog making it up into her nose: Not only was the dude pushing seventy, but he began his little speech by referring to Yellow's opponents as *gentlemen!*

"If you can't control yourselves," he continued, his white mustache twitching, "I'm going to have to ask you all to leave!"

You and what army, Rook said to herself, quoting the punch line of an old T'sentrati joke.

One of the toughs, a mean-looking little guy in a muscle shirt, had whipped out a throwing knife during the old man's attempted reprimand. He gave the knife a backhand toss now, sending it whizzing past the owner's head and straight into the plywood wall behind the stage.

"Mind your manners, Gramps!" the youth cautioned.

Rook sighed tiredly, swallowed the last two drops of her drink, and stood up from the table.

"Boy, you guys sure have guts," she told the gathered gang members. They turned slowly toward her as she knew they would, looks of disbelief on their faces. "Think you can handle her all by yourselves?"

This brought immediate catcalls and challenges from the rest of the room. Rook smiled for the audience's benefit and winked at the gang leader. She had been through scenes like this too often to count, and she knew the leader's type as well as she knew herself. She was confident she could take him, and that would eliminate the need to go one on one with the others. All she had to do was go after the leader's pride, and she had already made a good start in that direction. . . .

"Blondie, take my advice and stay out of this or you'll be next," he warned her.

Rook looked away nonchalantly. "Maybe if two of you held her down while the others ran for reinforcements . . . Then you might have a chance."

The catcalls increased in volume and originality. Even the leader cracked an appreciative smile. He steadied his shades and gave Rook the once-over. "A comedian." He sneered. "Too bad for you I've got such a poor sense of humor, 'cause I'm gonna make you sorry you ever walked in here."

The nasty little knife thrower produced a second shiv, but the leader motioned him back. "She's mine," he told his boys, and launched himself into a charge.

Rook had plenty of time to prepare and position herself; plus she had already sized up the guy's strengths and weaknesses. He was coming at her full force, yelling at the top of his lungs, his hands at shoulder height slightly out front. On the balls of her feet now, Rook dropped herself into a crouch and brought her right arm in front of her face, elbow pointed outward. When the leader was within range, she twisted back, then sprang up and took her shot, catching the man square in the larynx.

Instantly, he went down on his knees, hands clutching his throat. "You almost killed me," he managed to rasp.

"Well, come at me again and let's see if I can get it right this time," Rook answered him.

The room was full of applause and cheers by now; even some of the gang members were laughing.

Rook heard Yellow Dancer say, "I think the baboon's overmatched," just before the leader growled and shouted, "Stop laughing!"

Then the knife wielder started to move in ...

Outside the bar, two Cyclones were added to the long row of cycles and various hybrid vehicles that lined the town's main street. Scott and Rand glanced at the cycles and at the bar and traded questioning looks.

"Shall we go in?" Rand asked.

Scott shrugged and removed his helmet. "What've we got to lose?"

"That's not what I wanted to hear," Rand started to say, but Annie was already off the Cyclone and heading for the door.

"Come on, Rand. I'm dry enough to spit cotton."

Rand exhaled forcibly and dismounted wondering just how he had let things get so out of hand. *Just one more town*, he had told himself. A place where he could feel all right about leaving Annie and saying a final farewell to Scott. Then it was going to be back to solo riding and the open road. But that had been three days and several towns ago, not one of which suited his needs. Nor did he have especially good feelings about this one. Two rows of ruined high-tech prefabs split by the northern highway and squeezed between the stone walls of an arid canyon, the place had a filthy, forlorn look to it. It seemed as though the town had surrendered long before the Invid's arrival.

"They could at least clean the place up," Rand said to Scott now. "Bunch of lazy slobs. . . ."

"You country boys do things differently, I suppose," Scott said in a patronizing way.

Rand scowled. "At least we have enough self-respect

to keep our homes from becoming pigsties. You wonder why I'd rather live off the land, Scott? Well, look around."

"Oh, quit arguing, you two," Annie said, stepping through the barroom's swinging doors. "This dump isn't so bad. What do you think they do for fun around here?"

Inside, the first thing that greeted their eyes was a knife fight.

An attractive young woman in a red bodysuit was squaring off against a mean-looking youth wielding what looked like a hunting knife. Onlookers were cheering and offering words of encouragement to both parties. On the room's stage, a tall, lean female and a white-haired old man yelled for the fight to stop.

Scott stopped short. "It's her!?"

"Who?" said Annie.

"She's the one who helped us out the other day—the girl on the Cyclone!"

Rand's eyes went wide. "The *girl* on the Cyclone? Now you tell me!... Well what are we waiting for? Let's go—"

"No, hold up a minute." Scott put his arm out to restrain Rand. "I'm sure she can handle herself all right."

"But they'll kill her," said Annie.

Scott shook his head. "No, I don't think so."

Rand decided that Scott might be right. The woman moved like a dancer, dodging the youth's every thrust and overhand, her blond hair twirling about her face. One of the other men in the crowd was urging the knifer on with threats of his own.

"Stop your prancin' around! Stick her, man! Stick her!"

But the woman wasn't about to let that happen. She backed away with calculated deliberation, turning and folding at just the right moments. Rand could see that the rogue was losing patience and getting sloppy with his cover; he also noted that this was not lost on the woman in red. She set herself, legs wide, and waited for him to come in. Sure enough, the youth tried an over-the-top reverse and left himself wide open; the woman spun out from under it and completed her turn with a roundhouse kick that nailed him across the face, throwing him against one of the tables. The knifer went down as the table collapsed under him, but a second man, a large, dark-skinned tough wearing an earflapped cap, caught the woman from behind in a full nelson. She tried to struggle free but found herself overpowered. At the same time a third member of the gang sauntered in and took the knife from his fallen comrade. He tapped the tip of the blade menacingly against the woman's cheek.

"You can say good-bye to that pretty face of yours, sister," Rand heard the man say.

Scott was already stepping in, as was the female singer, who had started to grab for the knife stuck in the wall behind the stage. But Rand moved quicker than both of them: He swept up a heavy half-empty goblet from a nearby table and hurled it, knocking the knife from the gang leader's hand. As the youth screamed and dropped, holding his struck hand, Rand yelled, "Duck!" and launched a second glass.

Rook saw this one headed her way and stretched herself thin in the larger man's hold, arms fully extended as she slithered down. The glass hit the man in the face, and his hold on her collapsed; he was holding his nose and moaning when Rook brought her boot down onto his instep and turned away out of reach.

"I'm gonna kill you for that!" the man yelled. But when he took his hands away from his face, he found himself staring at Scott's drawn blaster.

"Get moving—all of you!" Scott told them.

Weapons were a common enough sight in the waste, but a blaster was seldom seen. Taken by surprise, the gang members began to back toward the swinging doors. "You win this one, soldier," the leader threw over his shoulder. "But the war's not over yet."

In a moment the sounds of revving and departing cycles filled the bar.

Rook looked disdainfully at her rescuers; she recognized them as the three she had saved from an Invid setup in Laako three days before. The redheaded one named Rand was eyeing her appreciatively.

"Why'd you have to butt in?" Rook said harshly, and left the bar.

"Guess there's no pleasing some people," Rand threw after her.

"Swelled head!" said Annie, making a face and gesturing.

"Well, I'm grateful for your help," said a lilting voice.

Rand turned and nearly fell over: It was *Yellow Dancer*! He hadn't recognized her before and could hardly believe his eyes now. "It can't be," he stammered, unable to control his excitement. "I've seen you at least twenty times, but I never thought I'd get the chance. . . ." He turned and made a desperate lunge for a napkin and shoved it toward Yellow. "I know it's silly, but . . . it's for my kid sister, you know?"

Yellow smiled knowingly. The bar owner took a pen from his jacket pocket and passed it to her. "To your kid sister," said Yellow, chuckling. "As always . . ."

Annie saw Scott's look of bewilderment and said, "It's Yellow Dancer. Haven't you ever heard of her?"

Scott smiled thinly and shook his head.

"Boy, you're really out of it, Scott."

Scott ignored the comment and turned to the owner. "That gang, who are they?"

The man shrugged. "The usual riffraff. Their kind seem to be just about everywhere nowadays."

"Yes, but what about the local authorities—have you thought of asking them to do something?"

Rand raised his eyes to the ceiling in a dramatic gesture and turned away embarrassed.

The manager stared at Scott a moment, then said, "Mister, those *are* the local authorities."

CHAPTER
SIX

Tirolian society—that is, the generation of Terrans that grew to manhood and womanhood under T.R. Edwards, Dr. Emil Lang, and to some extent (by proxy, as it were), Admiral Rick and Commander Lisa Hunter—took a decidedly different course than its counterpart on Earth (under Chairman Moran, Supreme Commander Leonard, et al.). Thanks to Edwards's chauvinism, bigotry, and undisguised misogyny, one would certainly have been hard pressed to encounter the likes of a Dana Sterling or a Marie Crystal among the Tirolian contingent... Scott Bernard had been raised in such a milieu, and there were things, as well as attitudes, on Earth that he had never dreamed possible.

Xandu Reem, *A Stranger at Home: A Biography of Scott Bernard*

RINGO AND HIS BOYS ROARED AWAY FROM THE BAR and regrouped at the edge of town. Their cycles, one outfitted with a sidecar, were well equipped with weapons, and it would have been simple to blast and torch the bar; but that wasn't really an option: Pops' had the coldest beer within three hundred miles. So they decided to turn their frustrations against any newcomers who might wander into town; a bit of the old ultraviolence, as it had once been called. Instead, however, they soon found an even more suitable target in the form of the ex-soldier named Lunk, who had been in town on and off for the past two months. More than once Ringo had attempted to goad the man into a fight with less than satisfying results. The attempts had increased in frequency once Ringo found out something about Lunk's recent military past, but still he was unable to push the man into a hand-to-hand confrontation.

But now, after his humiliating run-in with the strangers in the bar, Ringo was in no mood for subtlety or verbal provocation. No sooner had Lunk's battered six-wheel personnel carrier lumbered by the gang's edge-of-town position than Ringo ordered his men into pursuit. There was nothing like a little manhunting to pick you up when you were feeling down.

Lunk was twenty-five, a huge, barrel-chested man with almost brutish facial features: a wide, prominent chin, heavy-lidded, soulful eyes, and a broad, flat nose. He had let his hair grow long these past few months and kept it out of his face with a yellow elastic headband. His size alone would have given most men pause, but there was something soft and secretive about him that often allowed smaller aggressive types to feel they could have a free hand with him.

One look at Ringo's impromptu roadside gathering and Lunk knew that he was in for it; he told his companion, Kevin, to hang on and began to push the ancient APC along the town's main street for all it was worth.

He could see four cycles in the carrier's circular outboard rearview mirrors now; Ringo's men were opening up with handlebar and faring-mounted weapons, toying with him as he swerved the heavy vehicle left and right.

"How many of them are there?!" Kevin asked in a panic from the shotgun seat.

"Too many!" Lunk yelled back as machine-gun rounds fractured the mirrors.

Two rockets exploded in the street in front of the APC, and Lunk braked hard, losing control. The vehicle slid off the roadway and crashed into an enormous pile of debris that had been 'dozed away from a fallen storefront. The impact left Lunk and Kevin momentarily stunned, but they quickly shook themselves out of it and scampered out of the carrier's open top, taking careless and crazed giant strides down the back side of the heap.

Ringo and his boys threw their bikes into the pile with equal abandon, launching themselves over the top only to career down the rear face, laughing maniacally all the while. Lunk and Kevin had taken an alleyway that led to the main street, so Ringo ordered his gang to split up, sending the sidecar cyclist one way and instructing the others to form up on his lead.

Lunk wasn't aware of the trap until he saw the sidecar skid around a corner and head his way. Turning, he heard Ringo and the rest of the bikes behind him. He shoved Kevin toward the debris-strewn sidewalk, hoping they would be able to make it into one of the abandoned buildings, but at the same moment the sidecar driver gunned it and came down on them. One of Ringo's gang —a dark-skinned dude every inch as big as Lunk— leaned out from the sidecar seat and made a grab for Kevin. Lunk flattened himself against the street, but Kevin sidestepped too late. Ringo's man managed to get a handful of shirt and shoulder, and by the time Lunk looked up, Kevin was being dragged down the street by the cycle.

Lunk heard him scream for help but could do nothing; Ringo's men were accelerating toward him now, shouting and yahooing. Lunk spun around and ran toward Pops' bar. Halfway there, the sound of the cycles ringing in his ears, Lunk noticed that a group of men and women were gathered out front. And one of them was raising a weapon of some kind. . . .

He dropped himself into a tuck-and-roll seconds before the weapon fired. The round impacted against an unbraced section of heaped-up vehicles and mecha parts and loosed some of it into a slide. Lunk heard shouts and the squeal of brakes behind him. One of the bikes went down, sliding uncontrolled along the street with a rasping, scraping sound. Lunk reached Pops' just as Ringo's cycle pulled up, but the gang leader found himself confronting the man with the weapon.

"You again," Lunk heard Ringo seethe. "You're really pressing your luck, robby."

Hearing Ringo use the derisive slang term for a Robotech soldier, Lunk turned to study his rescuer. The man was straddling a Cyclone and wearing a uniform with patches Lunk couldn't identify. Nor was the weapon familiar.

"Put your hands where I can see them," the soldier told Ringo. "Now turn your cycles around and get out of here. The party's over."

Ringo adjusted his dark glasses and flashed one of his infamous grins. "Have it your way...." He looked over at Lunk. "If you wanna see your friend alive, come on out to the ranch—if you have the guts, that is!"

The three cycles roared off, and the soldier asked about Lunk's friend. Lunk quickly scanned the crowd: mostly locals he had seen before, but there were three or four he didn't recognize. Two attractive women and some carrot-topped kid. Another Cyclone rider. They were staring at him expectantly.

"Stay out of it," Lunk said, starting to walk off.

Spider stepped out of the crowd; they had ridden together previously, Spider, Lunk, and Kevin....

"Hey, Lunk, you're not going to just walk away?" Spider said to him questioningly. "We've gotta go get 'im, man. We can't leave him with Ringo!"

Lunk stopped, hung his head, then resumed his heavy steps.

"With a friend like you, a guy doesn't need enemies," the soldier called out to the delight of the crowd.

Lunk spun around, ashamed but angry; Spider and the others were still waiting.

"All right," the soldier was saying, strapping on some

sort of pectoral armor. "Where's this ranch? How far is it from here?"

"About five miles—" Pops started to say, but the soldier's younger companion interrupted.

"Hang on a minute, Scott," the redhead said. "You can't keep fighting everybody's battles for them. You think you're going to whip the whole planet back into shape single-handed, and I think you're nuts!"

"I wouldn't advise tangling with Ringo, stranger," Pops added. "Just take our thanks and ride on out of here."

But Scott didn't answer either of them. He put his helmet on, started the Cyclone, and wheeled off. A woman in similar armor riding a red mecha followed him. Lunk heard the soldier's companion mutter a curse and yell for Scott to slow down; then he angrily straddled his own Cyclone and joined the others.

"Lunk..." Spider said leadingly.

Lunk spun around, a determined look on his face now. "All right, let's go."

"Really?"

"I won't let those bums make a chump outta me, Spider. Kevin's our friend, and we can't leave him out there." Lunk turned to the crowd. "I need some wheels. I've got scrip enough to rent 'em."

"Take mine," said Pops, fishing keys out of his shirt pocket. "And don't worry about paying me, either."

Lunk caught the tossed chain, threw a thanks over his shoulder, and ran over to Pops' olive-drab tri-wheel. Spider straddled the rear seat. Lunk noticed that the tall woman singer he had seen once or twice in the bar was also headed toward her vehicle. Meanwhile, the little kid with the E.T. cap was beside him, introducing herself as Annie.

"Are you married by any chance?" she asked Lunk.

Lunk's face twisted up in shock. "What, are you kid-din'?"

Annie threw open her arms and said, "You lucky boy!" as Lunk rode off, a look of bewilderment on his face. "The man of my dreams," she added a moment later, climbing into Yellow Dancer's pink roll-barred jeep.

Scott's improvised posse of seven followed the road out of town to a turnoff that wound up into the hills. They stopped once so that Scott and Rook could suit Rand up in Cyclone armor and run him quickly through the basics of mechamorphosis.

The ranch sat at the crest of a gentle rise near a wide stream that made it one of the choicest spots in the district. It was enclosed by a rustic post-and-rail fence, and there were patches of grass and a few beautiful old trees that had weathered more storms, natural and otherwise, than anyone cared to guess. Scott and company rode in without ceremony and found Ringo's gang waiting for them in the shade of an immense oak. There were five of them: the knife-wielding punk, the hulk, and two others who had been with Ringo in the bar earlier that day. They were all astride their bikes—the hulk in his usual sidecar seat—grouped close together in a shallow arc, cycle weapons pointed outward. Kevin was behind them, lashed by thick rope to the tree trunk.

Scott ordered his group to a halt two hundred yards from the tree. Ringo's group wouldn't have stood a chance against the firepower of one Cyclone, let alone three, but it was obvious from the start that Ringo wanted to go one on one with Lunk. Kevin's precarious position guaranteed against any Cyclone fireworks, so in a certain sense (as was always the case when hostages were involved) Scott's position was the more vulnerable one.

Lunk was aware of what was going down and asked Spider to climb off the triple-wheeler. It was likely, given Ringo's flair for dramatics, that he would begin the festivities with a bike joust, and Lunk figured he could handle the thing better if he was alone.

"Okay, but be careful," Spider said, stepping away.

Lunk snorted. "I'm sick to death of being careful."

Rand and Rook were side by side a few yards away, with Scott slightly off to one side behind them. "I can't figure out why you came," Rand was saying to the red Cyclone rider through the helmet. "You've got no stake in this."

"I've got just as much reason to be here as you," Rook said harshly without looking over at him.

"Everybody stay loose," Scott warned. "Keep your fingers away from the triggers. I don't want anyone getting hurt unless it can't be helped."

"No great loss, if you ask me," Rook muttered.

Rand glanced over at her. "Reminds me of a movie I saw once. *Gunfight at the* . . . I can't remember the title. But what happens is that—"

"People die in real life, pal. Keep that in mind."

Before Rand could say anything, Ringo called out: "Hey, Lunky-boy—I can hear your knees knockin' together! Is it gonna be just you and me, or do you need the army behind you?" Ringo's gang hooted and howled. "I mean, you didn't have much use for the army a while ago, did ya? In fact, you got a history of runnin' away from fights, the way I hear it. Ain't that right?"

Lunk gritted his teeth. Sweat was beading up across his face, and indeed, his knees were knocking against the valve covers of the cycle's engine. "You don't know nothin' about it, ya little shit!" he managed to bite out.

Ringo laughed and slapped his knee. "Sorry if I blew your cover. I keep forgettin' you're too modest to brag about your military record!"

"What're you trying to prove?" Lunk yelled, muscles and veins standing out like cords in his beefy neck.

"Nothin'," Ringo returned. "Nothin' at all. 'Cept the Invid *hate* soldiers, and since we don't have much use for them ourselves, we decided to help them along this time."

Lunk began to rev his cycle, but Scott gestured to him to hold his ground. "Hand over your hostage!" Scott demanded of Ringo.

The gang leader turned to his men and laughed. "We might just make you part of today's quota, robby!"

"Yeah, we ain't picky!" the knifer threw in.

"And we're not afraid of your firepower, neither," the hulk yelled from the sidecar, raising a bazooka-type weapon into view.

"They're psyching themselves up," Rook cautioned the others. "Be ready!"

On Ringo's word the four cycles leapt forward in a charge, but all at once a round detonated in their midst, throwing some of them off their machines. Scott, Rand, and Rook exchanged looks, wondering who had fired. Then they heard Spider and Annie's simultaneous screams and looked up: Three Invid Shock Troopers had appeared over the canopy of the oak tree. Ringo and his boys were bolting for the shelter of the ranch house as continued flashes from the Troopers' shoulder cannons shook the ground and blew their cycles apart. Kevin was trying desperately to free himself from the tree trunk, and Annie was shouting, "Do something!"

Scott took the initiative and shot his Cyclone forward, engaging the thrusters and going to Battle Armor mode as the mecha left the ground. Two of the Invid went after him, while the third dropped in low toward Lunk and the others. Rand was working the system switches frantically, eager for the mecha to reconfigure.

"Come on! Come on!... What the heck's wrong with this thing!?" he said to Rook.

"Just calm down," she told him. "Remember what Scott told you—your thoughts have to help it along. Relax and stop bashing away at it." Rook lowered her head and threw the thumb switch. Rand watched amazed as the cycle restructured, wrapping itself around her and integrating with her armor. "Treat it gently—like it's alive," Rook added, standing now.

Scott meanwhile was off in another part of the grassy fields dancing between the annihilation discs sent his way by the Troopers who had put down on either side of him. Lunk saw him lift off after half a dozen agile leaps and bounces and return fire from the suit's forearm rocket launchers.

"I can't escape it!" Lunk yelled to no one in particular. "I thought I'd never be fighting again!"

Rook was engaging the third Invid, while Rand continued to struggle with reconfiguration. He was about to give up on it, when he felt the mecha's reciprocal vibe, and suddenly the damned thing was actually conforming itself to his armor. He stood up, showing a look of disbelief under the helmet's faceplate, and gently engaged the system's hoverthrusters, searching the skies for signs of Rook or Scott. At last he saw the red Cyclone rider. She was powering up through a backflip one minute and dropping like a stiff-legged bomb the next. But her Invid target leapt away in time, hooking itself overhead and dishing out a blast that nearly caught her. She avoided the explosion by launching straight up, but the Trooper was sticking close, discharging two more bolts, one of which nicked her armor and sent her into a spinning descent toward a stand of trees.

Scott was handling himself well against the other two Troopers but had yet to land a Scorpion on either of them. He was down on the ground now, getting off another shot before the Invid surrounded him, pincers swinging, discs cratering the soft earth. Rand joined him, and together they managed to chase the Troopers off momentarily.

Scott was congratulating Rand on his mechamorphosis when Lunk pulled up alongside on the triple-wheeler.

"You weren't ever a member of the space battalion, were you?" Lunk asked Scott.

"Yeah? . . ." said Scott. "So what?"

"Then you can fly a Veritech."

"Of course I can," Scott said excitedly. "Do you have one?"

Lunk nodded. "Follow me."

Rand watched them zoom off, Scott running alongside Lunk's cycle. He dodged an Invid that attempted to flatten him into the ground and brought his forearm up to fire. But the Trooper was already flying off to link up with the other two, all three headed in the same general direction as Lunk and Scott.

If I hang around with this guy long enough, I'm gonna get myself killed for sure, Rand said to himself.

Then Rook was suddenly beside him, upright in Battle Armor mode and hovering two feet off the ground. "What's the matter," she asked him, "your joints rusting up on you or something?"

"No, I was just trying to—"

"You really aren't much use in combat, are you?"

"Hey, wait a minute!" Rand shouted as she began to hover off in the same configuration. "It's not like I'm *supposed* to be here, you know. I mean, technically I'm a noncombatant, did you know that? Did I ever tell you about the time I fought off three Invid patrols at the same time . . . ?"

From the cover of the ranch house, Ringo watched Spider set Kevin free from the ropes that held him to the tree. Knifer was kneeling by the window, peering over the stool; the hulk was cowering in a corner under a shelf.

"Stop your whinin', you lily-livered rogue!" Ringo shouted from the window.

Knifer looked up. "Hey, Ringo, I think I can hear *your* knees knockin'."

Ringo made an exasperated face and brought his fist down on Knifer's skull. "It's because I'm *mad,* bonehead. Mad, mad, mad!" He punctuated each word with a follow-up blow.

Elsewhere, Annie was asking Yellow Dancer why she was hanging around. They were in the singer's pink armored vehicle, parked some distance from the scene of the initial fighting. "What do you want from them?" Annie wanted to know. "I'm warning you, I can get very jealous."

Yellow turned to her from the driver's seat with an enigmatic smile. "Believe me," she assured Annie, "there's absolutely nothing for you to be jealous of."

"Well, then, it's okay," Annie said, perking up. "You can hang around as much as you want."

The Veritech hangar was a dilapidated circular building, holed in numerous places, with a hemispherical red roof sectioned off and reinforced by curved trusses. A mostly ruined solar windmill rose alongside the structure, which Scott guessed was a barn of some sort. Up ahead, he saw Lunk give a wave, jump the triple-wheeler from the top of a small grassy embankment, and accelerate through the fallow fields that led to the makeshift hangar. The Invid Shock Troopers were in hot pursuit overhead, their gleaming crablike bodies filling the sky.

"Hurry!" Scott could hear Lunk shout.

Scott had been expecting to find the rusting shell of a first-generation Veritech, but once inside the building his hopes took a leap forward. Carefully positioned in the spacious loft was what looked to be a well-maintained Alpha Fighter, sans augmentation pack and boosters, and certainly a leftover from the latter stages of the Second Robotech War.

"Climb in," said Lunk. "She's ready to fly."

"Who's been maintaining it?" Scott asked as he struggled out of the reconfigured Cyclone.

"Listen, I'm not as stupid as you might think," Lunk said, raising his voice above explosive volleys from the Invid. Discs were striking the fields nearby, loosening dirt and debris from the exposed rafters. "I was a certified bio-maintenance engineer. Trust me, this baby will fly like a dream."

Scott climbed into the barn loft and gave the Veritech's radome an affectionate pat. He threw himself up to the open canopy, got a good handhold, and slipped into the cockpit. He hadn't bothered to change out of the Cyclone armor, but now he exchanged his helmet for the Veritech's own "thinking cap" and began a run-through of the systems. It was so long since he had piloted a VT in atmosphere, he wondered if he could bring it off now.

"Everything seems in order!" he called down to Lunk as an explosion tore out a huge section of wall.

Lunk's hands went to his ears, and he threw himself to cover. Through the breach in the wall, Scott glimpsed the three Troopers land and begin their approach on the barn. *I'll never be able to power up fast enough to get out of here!* he thought.

But just then Rand and Rook arrived to check the aliens' advance. The red Cycloner launched herself like a projectile straight into one of the Trooper's optic sensors, while Rand fired two Scorpions against a second. It was all the time Scott needed to bring up the Protoculture levels of the Veritech, and a moment later, much to

Rand's consternation, the radome of the VT was punching through the barn's roof.

Scott threw the VT into a steep climb, luring the Troopers away from their swipe attacks against Rook and Rand. Rand watched the fighter accelerate through a sweeping arc and head back into the faces of its pursuers, destroying one with a missile too swift for his eyes to track. But that was only the beginning: Now the fighter was reconfiguring to Battloid mode and leading the two remaining Invid on a high-speed chase over the countryside.

Scott thought the ship upright—a techno-knight standing in thin air—while salvos of annihilation discs beamed past him. He reached out, throwing levers that opened the missile compartments built into the Battloid's forearm, shoulder, and lower-leg armor, and thought the systems through to launch. It was all coming back to him now—*it had to!* For a moment, the techno-knight was encompassed in energy balloons; then dozens of missiles tore from their launch racks like so many red-tipped arrows of death. The Troopers took the full storm and were all but disintegrated by the force of the blasts.

Down below, Kevin and Spider were running toward the barn, a few steps ahead of Annie, who had just leapt from Yellow's jeep and was calling out for Lunk. Rook and Rand had already reconfigured their Cyclones and were doffing the hot and cumbersome battle armor when Scott brought the VT down, cut the engines, and threw open the canopy.

Lunk stepped from the barn unharmed and caught Annie midair as she jumped up and threw her arms around his neck. "There you are!" she gushed. "I knew they wouldn't get you, I knew you'd come back to me!"

Lunk held her away, offering a miffed but understanding grin.

"I've decided you're the only one for me!"

"Well, thanks," said Lunk. "I wish I could say the same." He smiled tolerantly and gently lowered Annie to the ground. "You're a little young for me...And besides, I've got other plans."

Annie stared up at him, despondent, and asked what those other plans might be.

Lunk threw his massive shoulders back. "Join the resistance," he said to all of them. "See if I can make up for past mistakes."

"I'd be glad to join forces with you, Lunk," said Scott. "If you mean what you say..."

Kevin looked from one to the other. "He's not serious, robby. Are you, Lunk?"

Lunk nodded. "I'm sick of sneakin' around like a frightened little weasel. Face it, Kevin, I'm a *soldier,* after all. And it's time I started acting like one."

"Use your head, Lunk," Kevin countered. "This war's a lost cause. What can two, ten, or even two hundred do against the Invid?"

"We can try," said Lunk.

Annie made a disappointed sound and turned her back to Lunk, hands behind her head. "And I thought you were special..."

Lunk bent down, perplexed, to ask: "But a minute ago I was the man of your dreams, remember?"

Annie's lips tightened, and she shook her head. "A long time ago I decided I'd never marry a soldier. They don't last long enough nowadays."

Kevin and Spider laughed.

"The kid's no dummy, that's for sure," Rand offered.

Yellow stepped down from the jeep and approached the VT. "I'd like to sign up for the team, Scott."

Rook sent a knowing elbow into Rand's ribs at the

same time Kevin sent one into Spider's. But Scott's answer disappointed all of them.

"Thanks," he said from the cockpit. "But we don't have enough troops yet to hire an entertainer."

"There's a lot more to me than meets the eye," said Yellow.

"As if that isn't enough," Rand commented under his breath but loudly enough for Rook to hear.

"All I see is an attractive woman in a rather slinky outfit," said Scott.

"Wrong on both counts," Yellow answered him, walking back to the jeep. "I've got something to show you."

A buzz of general puzzlement swept through the would-be team as Yellow sauntered off, especially when she turned her back to them and began to undo the rear buttons of her strapless top.

"Hey, w-wait a minute," Scott stammered in protest. "I appreciate your wanting to, er—*show* me, but don't think for a moment that's going to change my mind. . . ."

"Is she going to do what I think she's going to do?" said Annie, gulping.

"Sure looks that way," Rook said in an interested way.

Yellow meanwhile had removed her top and tossed it into the open jeep. She still had her back to them, long lavender hair falling all the way to the narrow band of her brassiere.

"H-hey, now hold on!" Rand said with a desperate tone.

Lunk laughed. "Well, she's right about one thing— she's not wearin' no slinky outfit anymore."

Yellow turned to throw them a wink over her shoulder, then reached back the way only a woman can and unfastened the bra, letting it slip from her breasts. She still had her back to them when she undid her trousers and let them fall. The pink jeep concealed whatever treasures these moments might have held for the red-faced team.

"*Now* what's she doing?" Lunk said as Dancer picked up a towel and began to scrub her face with it.

"I don't know," Scott responded sternly. "But I want an end to it right now, hear me, Yellow? You can stop this little game, because we're not taking you with us, and that's final!"

Then Yellow swung around to face them.

And something was wrong, very wrong, indeed.

"Oh, no!" Rook screamed, and began to laugh hysterically.

"Y-yellow Dancer?" Rand said tentatively.

Lunk, Kevin, and Spider drew in stunned but disappointed intakes of breath. Annie was simply confused; Scott, wordless. It was plain enough to see that Yellow Dancer was a man—a tall, rather hairless, lean and attractive man.

"You can start by calling me Lancer," he told his stunned audience, his voice deeper now. "I think the name suits me a little better. So, I hope there are no further objections to my tagging along with you."

"Well, I don't know..." Scott started to say. Woman or cross-dresser, what was the difference? he asked himself. But looking down at Rook now, he began to have second thoughts about all of this. Earth was a fascinating but bizarre place where women seemed to want to mix it up as much as the men. So maybe there was a place for her, er, *him*.

Rand meanwhile was beside himself. There were all those dreams of Yellow Dancer he had lived with for months—all those *fantasies*! "It can't *be*!" he was saying. "How could you do this to me—your biggest fan?!"

"I wasn't exactly thinking about you, Rand," Lancer said.

"Yeah," Rook chimed in. "Not like *he* was thinking about *you*!"

Everyone laughed, except Lancer. "So how about it, Captain? Do I make the team or not?"

Scott and Lunk exchanged looks and shrugs. "Yes," Scott said at last. "I guess you do."

CHAPTER
SEVEN

Mom, who thrived on adversity, had met her perfect foil in Rand. Fortunately for me, they eventually worked it through.

Maria Bartley-Rand, *Flower of Life: Journey Beyond Protoculture*

A TEAM HAD BEEN FORMED: SCOTT, RAND, ROOK, Annie, Lunk, and Lancer (although Scott wondered if the singer shouldn't be counted twice). None of them promised to accompany Scott all the way to Reflex Point—if such a place actually existed; it was simply a loose agreement among six people headed in the same general direction, each with a separate purpose in mind. Scott wanted to see the Invid defeated; at the very least he hoped to link up with other downed fighters from the Mars Division and establish an organized resistance. Lunk was searching for a redemption of sorts; Annie, for a family. But the aims of the others were less clear-cut; their pasts remained unrevealed, their motives somewhat suspect. Nevertheless, Scott had himself a team.

All he needed now was an adequate plan.

The present one wasn't working well at all. Rather than risk calling attention to their latest acquisition—the Alpha Fighter Lunk had so reverently maintained after his rather hasty departure from the Army of the Southern Cross—Scott and Lancer had flown the mecha north under the cover of night and secluded it along the river that marked the border of the neighboring territory. Lancer was to remain with the Veritech while Scott rode back to town on his Cyclone to collect the others. In the meantime, Lunk and Annie would be in charge of gathering up what they could in the way of supplies and foodstuffs. Rand and Rook would secure a safe route out for the loaded APC.

Things went smoothly enough at first; Lunk had seen to his assignment, and Scott rendezvoused with the APC/Cyclone convoy on schedule. They had begun their trek north and entered the highlands when the Invid appeared. It hadn't paid to leave enemies the likes of Ringo behind. . . .

Scott held the lead up the rugged mountain road; Rand and Annie were a few lengths behind, then came Lunk in the APC and Rook on her red Cyclone. There were at least five Troopers in pursuit, with annihilation discs striking the cliff faces above and below the roadway.

Scott waved for the others to pour it on and accelerated along the arid slope.

Rook pulled alongside him and shouted above the deafening explosions. "They're gaining on us!" To maintain their low profile, they had opted against suiting up in helmets or battle armor.

"We haven't got a prayer unless we can reach the Alpha." Scott turned to Rand, who had come up on the inside, and told him to take the lead. He and Rook would stay behind to armor up and reconfigure for combat.

Rand signaled his assent, cautioned Annie to hold

tight, and moved out front. But no sooner had they reached the crest than two Invid rose into view. Rand engaged the brakes, pivoting the mecha through a clean 180, and headed back down the hill.

Scott hadn't even dismounted yet. "Why are you turning around?" he shouted.

"They've got us surrounded," Rand reported. "We'd better go cross-country." He indicated the steep grade above the roadway and lowered his goggles.

"No. No detours," Scott argued. "The Alpha's only a few miles down the road—we've got to break through!"

Rand snorted and shook his head. "*You* break through, Captain. I'm heading for the hills." He stomped the Cyclone into gear and took off, scrambling up the rutted incline, heedless of Scott's shouts to stop. But not a moment later, Invid Troopers were ascending into view at both ends of the road, and Scott saw the logic of Rand's choice. He gestured to Rook and Lunk and screeched off up the hill.

There was a barren stretch of plateau at the top of the slope, separated from twin fingers of pine forest by steep crevices too wide to jump. The Invid Troopers realized their advantage and began to loose disc storms of energy from their cannons. As always, there seemed to be an effort made to incapacitate rather than kill the humans, but it could just as easily have been poor marksmanship on their part. In any case, the plateau—great swirls of weathered rock and shale—was being torn up and superheated by the Troopers' fusillades. Lunk's APC, slower and far less maneuverable than the Cyclones, provided the best target, and the Invid were soon concentrating their bursts against it. Inside the cab, the big man was bouncing around like a featherweight, barely in control of the thing anymore. When a blinding disc streaked by inches from the carrier, he lost it completely; the APC crashed into a boulder and overturned, hurling

Lunk twenty feet to a hard landing facedown on the shale. At the last instant, however, he had grabbed two sacks of supplies and had managed to hold on to them during his brief airborne journey. The sacks cushioned his fall somewhat, but he blacked out momentarily nevertheless. Coming to, he heard Rook's voice behind him, warning him to keep his head down. He did as instructed and *felt* rather than saw the red Cyclone streak over him.

Scott and Rand had witnessed the collision and stopped their Cyclones to return fire against the Troopers, bringing rear weapons into play. Behind them, Lunk was attempting to gather together and rebag items spilled from the sacks.

"Lunk! Forget that stuff and come on!" Scott shouted.

"But we need these Protoculture energy cells for the mecha!" Lunk countered, ducking as a series of annihilation discs Frisbeed overhead. The Invid were close at hand now, upright and laying out salvo after salvo of white-hot fire. Explosions began to erupt all around him, orange blossoms in the shale, and he was forced to abandon the supplies. He made a beeline for Scott's idling Cyclone, straddling the rear seat not a moment too soon.

"My toothbrush!" Lunk moaned, looking back at the wrecked APC as Scott gunned the mecha into a wheelie.

"So your teeth will fall out," Scott said into the wind. "It's better than having your head blown off."

They were headed downhill a moment later, across a smooth flow of solid rock with an inviting forest of tall firs and eucalyptis at its base. As they neared the trees, Scott spied an unpaved road and made for it, signaling the others to follow his lead.

Two of the Invid attempted to track them but eventually gave up; it was widely believed (but certainly unproven) that the Invid had a kind of fearsome respect for forests in general. The Troopers circled overhead for a long while, then began to fan out trying to cover all possible points of egress. Meanwhile, Scott directed his band north in an effort to strike the river. By his reckoning, they were now somewhat west of Lancer and the Veritech, but reaching the river would put them in good position for a direct eastward swing.

The forest thinned as they worked their way north, giving way to a series of tall grass terraces that dropped in measured steps to the river gorge itself. The grass was deep enough to offer places of concealment for themselves as well as the Cyclones, so they continued their cautious advance. There was no sign of the enemy.

"Do you think we lost 'em?" Lunk asked, poking his head above the grass. He could see tall buttes and stone tors in the distance.

Rand answered him from nearby. "We must have—there's no way those things can follow a trail through the woods. Believe me, I know."

"How 'bout some food, then?"

Rook showed herself. "You really take the cake, Lunk."

"I wish I could—"

"First you nearly get us all killed, and now all you can think about is that selfish stomach of yours!"

"Drop it!" Scott said more harshly than was necessary. He switched on his Cyclone briefly to read the system indicator displays. "You were right about those Protoculture cells, Lunk," he admitted. "It's imperative that I get back to the Alpha. Someone's going to have to draw the Invid off in case I'm spotted. We can't let them find the ship."

Rand suddenly shushed him. "They're coming," he whispered.

The team dropped themselves into the grass, raising weapons as they did so. Minutes later, three Troopers could be seen patrolling the gorge, their scanners alert for movement on the cliffs above the river.

"Everybody hold your fire," said Scott.

"How did they find us?" Rand said to no one in particular.

Annie put her hands to her breast. "I betcha they heard the sound of my heart pounding."

Rand stared down at the Mars-galant Scott had given him earlier; it was a long-barreled version of the sidearm blaster the offworlder wore, shaped a bit like an elongated closed-topped Y. *Time to go on-line with this thing,* he said to himself. But no sooner did he flip the switch than the Troopers stopped their bipedal patrol and turned on them.

"Open fire!" Scott yelled as globes of fulgent energy formed at the muzzles of the Troopers' cannons.

Lunk, Rook, and Rand stood up, bringing their H–90's to bear against the invaders. Phased-laser fire seared into the Troopers' armored bodies, while annihilation discs ripped into the cliff's grassy terrace, touching off violent fires and clouds of dense smoke. Two more Invid appeared above the cliffs behind the team, adding their own volleys to the arena.

"We've gotta get back to the trees!" Rand shouted above the angry buzz of disc fire and concussive detonations.

"Lead them away from the Alpha!" said Scott.

"*You* worry about the Alpha. I'm gone!"

Abandoning their Cyclones, the team broke ranks and began to belly-crawl their way through the grass back toward the tree line. They scaled slope after slope, beating a circuitous retreat across each terrace. The closest call came when Rook miscalculated and nearly slipped into a narrow ravine; but Rand was there for her, hauling her up and supporting her while they ran. In the forest once more, they took to the trees and hid themselves high up in the branches. Invid Troopers were walking sweeping patrols along the perimeter; two were actually braving the cool and dark mystery to probe deep into the woods. Rand flicked his gallant on-line again as one of the latter group was passing beneath him. Curiously, the Invid stopped short, its would-be head rotating upward.

Rand took a sudden, sharp intake of breath—not out of fear but from realization. *Of course!* he told himself. *At the river they stopped when I activated the power cell on my blaster. And just now . . .*

It made sense, but it was time to try an experiment to validate his findings: He disarmed the power cell, and sure enough, the Invid lost interest and stomped off. "Yeah, that's gotta be it," Rand said softly. He was exhaling pent-up fear when something orange and menacing suddenly dropped on him from the branch above. His throat refused to utter the scream his guts demanded, but he gave a start nonetheless, raising the weapon like a club, only to realize that it was Annie, upside down and dangling from her knees, carrot-colored hair like an unfurled flag.

"Were you talking to yourself?" she demanded. "Were you? Huh?"

"Don't *ever* sneak up on me!" Rand seethed.

Scott, Rook, and Lunk were on the ground now, telling Rand that the coast was clear. Excitedly, Rand scrambled down out of the tree.

"I think I know why we've been having so much trouble getting these blasted walking lobsters off our trail," he announced. He gestured to the weapon's on-line switch. "We've been giving ourselves away every time we switch on our Cyclones or our blasters."

"How so?" said Lunk.

"They can detect the bio-energy given off by our Robotech mecha."

Lunk helped Annie down from the tree. "You could

be right," he said to Rand. "Back at the river Scott left the panel gauges of his Cyclone on. They could've homed in on that."

"Right!" Rand agreed.

"It makes sense," said Scott. It had never been an issue on Tirol, but then, there were a lot of things about Earth that separated it from Tirol. . . .

"Of course it makes sense," Rand was continuing. "They thrive on Protoculture, right? Well, it's like they can *smell* the stuff, the same way a shark is able to smell blood in the water."

"Charming thought," Rook said distastefully.

Annie laughed. "Mr. Wizard! You really thought that out by yourself, huh?"

Rand smiled with elaborate modesty.

"Sure doesn't happen very often, does it?" Rook scoffed.

Rand whirled on her. "Yeah? Besides your looks, what have you contributed lately?"

Rook's nostrils flared. "All right, that does it! Let's step aside and settle this once and for all!"

"You sure you don't just want to get me alone in the bushes?" Rand said, smiling and stroking his chin. "Admit it—"

"Stop it!" Scott broke in, silencing the two of them. "Arguing among ourselves isn't going to help matters any. We're supposed to be friends, in case you've forgotten."

"Oh, is that so?" Rook said, arms akimbo. "Well, I don't remember him ever becoming a friend of mine," she threw to Rand.

"Then what the hell are you doing here?" Rand barked. "I didn't ask you along! We don't need this kind of nonsense."

Rook and Rand faced off defensively.

"Cool off," Lunk told everyone. "There'll be plenty

of time to scream at each other later. But right now we gotta get back to the Alpha."

"Kiss and make up," Annie said to Rand as Lunk walked off. "Or at least shake hands."

"Fine with me." Rand shrugged and glared at Rook. "But maybe you should ask the lady with the chip on her shoulder!"

Gradually, in single file, they began to work their way back to the river. Rook and Rand opened a second front in their war when Rook insisted that something was following them and Rand called her paranoid. Scott came down on them again and ordered Lunk to walk between them as a buffer. And it was in this way that the three men managed to avoid the leeches . . .

Scott and Rand heard Annie's scream and turned around in time to see the descent of the mutant worm rain. They dropped from the forest canopy, instantly attaching themselves to the two girls.

Lunk made a sound of disgust and backed away. "There's millions of them!"

Annie was crying and stamping her feet. Rook's face was contorted, her body shaking all over. "Do something!" she screamed to Rand, but he only smiled. "You creep! Get these things off me!" She stood paralyzed, as if not knowing where to begin—on her arms, her neck, her face . . . Just then another leech dropped from the trees and landed on her forehead; Rook screamed and collapsed to the ground, wailing and kicking her feet in frustration.

"Hold still," Scott said, kneeling alongside her and pulling the leeches off Rook's arm. But Rand stopped him before he had detached more than two or three. He took Lunk's lit cigarette and touched the lighted end to one of the creatures.

"Make things hot for them and they'll pop out on their own," he explained as the leech dropped off, sizzling.

"Pull them off and you end up leaving the sucker intact."
Methodically, he moved the cigarette from leech to
leech.

"I tell you, I get a real kick seeing city girls in the
country," Rand told Scott while he labored. "They look
so darn cute when they start screaming." He smiled at
Rook. "You should've seen yourself..."

She made a face, averting her gaze from Rand's hand-
iwork. "Can you blame me? It's *disgusting*." She shuddered. "I hate to break this to you, Daniel Boone, but
there's something called civilization out there. Maybe
you've heard of it."

Rand snorted. "That's where you have crime and
filth, right?"

"Better than slimy little blood-sucking tree leeches."

"Sourpuss," Rand said, standing up and moving over
to Annie. "Any leech that gets a good taste of you is
gonna swear off human beings forever."

Rook stood up, angry at first, then flashing an enigmatic, almost seductive smile. "We'll see..." she said,
walking off into the bushes to check for leeches off limits
to Rand's search.

They stuck to the forest this time rather than risk
showing themselves in the open ground that bordered
the river. Two hours along they stopped to rest below
the small falls of a tributary that fed the gorge. Rand
stripped a sapling of twigs and fashioned a fishing rod for
himself. He waded out to a rock midstream and cast in
his line. Scott and the others sat under the trees along
the bank.

"Hey, Rand," Annie taunted him. "Do you really
think you can catch anything with that funny-looking
stick of yours?"

Rand frowned while everyone had a good laugh. "Just

you wait," he told them. "I'm an expert, and if there's a trout anywhere in this river, it's mine."

It was a pleasant spot, full of water sounds, animal life, and cool shade stirred by a gentle breeze. "Almost makes you forget where you are," Scott mused.

Rook nodded absently. "I know. I'm starting to feel like we're at a Boy Scout picnic."

Rand meanwhile was addressing his would-be catch, when something small and mean hit him on the head. He looked around and found Lunk crouched on the limb of an overhanging tree. "Hey, what's the idea?" Rand started to ask.

"Invid . . ." Lunk said softly, cupping his hands to his mouth.

Scott, Annie, and Rook took to the cover of the brush. Rand was looking around for a place to hide when he noticed the line stretched taut. He grabbed hold of the anchored pole, ignoring Scott's orders to abandon the fish. It had to be a five-pounder at least, and he wasn't about to let it go. Even so, he could sense the ground-shaking approach of the Trooper. He pulled hard and saw the rainbow break water; it was bigger than he had thought. The Invid's cloven footfalls were increasing; Rand gave a mighty tug and brought the fish up. But just then the line snapped. At the same time the Trooper appeared through the trees.

Deciding it might behoove him to be the one that got away, Rand dropped the pole and dived from the rock.

Lunk was still in the tree, standing now, his back flattened against the trunk, when the Trooper passed. A second Trooper lumbered into view an instant later. Peering from the bushes, his H–90 raised, Scott saw that the two were headed toward the falls. Rand was nowhere to be seen.

Unless one happened to be a fish.

Running short on breath when the first Invid hit the

water, Rand had propelled himself downstream, hugging the rocky bottom, only to run into another pair of armored legs. His lungs were on fire, threatening to implode, but surfacing wouldn't necessarily improve the situation any. He swallowed hard, sensing a darkness creeping into the edges of his vision. . . .

The two Troopers stopped in the middle of the river and swung their sensors through a 360-degree scan. Concerned for Rand's safety, Scott ran from cover when the Invid had crossed the stream and moved off into the woods on the opposite bank.

Lunk dived in, and found his companion unconscious on the river bottom, arms still locked around the boulder he had hugged to keep himself submerged. He brought him up and laid him facedown on the bank; then straddled him and carefully began to use his big hands to pump water from Rand's lungs.

"Is he going to be all right?" Annie asked.

Scott nodded. "He just passed out."

Rand's color started to return, and he coughed up a few mouthfuls of water. Softly, Rook called his name.

Rand straightened up with an energy that surprised all of them, knocking an unsuspecting Lunk backward into the river. He looked around dazedly and dropped back to his knees exhausted.

"Uh, the Invid are all gone," Annie said.

"Yeah, you can calm down, Superman," Rook added.

Rand smiled thinly.

"All right," Scott said, extending his hand to Lunk and helping him to the bank. "Now that they're gone, we can get back to Lancer. We can't be too far—"

Rook saw Scott's eyes go wide. She spun around and saw the reason for it: An enormous black bear, frightened and up on its hind legs, was breaking through the brush. Scott had his weapon raised but froze as a bizarre giant tiger-striped spider dropped from a tree onto the weapon's barrel. Scott winced and uttered a startled cry, reflexively loosing a bolt from the thing that whizzed past the bear's head. Rook lunged for Annie as the animal's huge claw came down, narrowly missing her. Lunk almost caught the backlash and rolled for cover.

Rand missed with two shots from his own weapon, and the bear's right paw connected with the blaster, sending him and the weapon flying in opposite directions. Rand looked up into bared teeth and sharp claws, the face of furry black death. He made his peace with the Creator and glimpsed a brilliant flash of white light ... But when the smoke cleared, he found himself still alive and the bear gone—*vaporized*.

The only problem was that there was now an Invid ship overhead—and not one of the Troopers either, but one of the rust-brown Pincer units!

"Well, I never thought I'd be happy to see you guys!" Rand said as he got to his feet, the smell of roasted meat in the air. He joined the rest of the team in a jog for the woods.

The Invid rained fire down on them as they ran, steering them away from the safety of the trees and bringing one of the patrolling Troopers in on the action. The team soon found itself cornered, fenced in on open ground by high-energy beams and annihilation discs. But Scott heard a familiar sound cutting through the tumultuous roar of the Invid's death-rays.

It was Lancer, riding one of the abandoned Cyclones.

Lavender hair trailing in the wind, he leapt the mecha over a surprised Invid Trooper and landed it not more than fifteen feet from where the team stood huddled together.

"All I had to do was ride to the sound of the guns!"

Lancer yelled when the Cyclone had skidded to a halt. "What're you waiting for, Scott? Climb on!"

Scott offered a silent prayer to the gods who governed silver linings and threw himself onto the rear seat. Lancer popped the mecha into a long wheelie that shot them through the legs of the bewildered Trooper. But the Pincer ship chased them, loosing continuous disc fire from its treetop course.

Lancer kept the Cyclone in the woods for cover. Scott saw that they were nearing the river gorge now and raised himself on the rear pegs in an effort to spot the Alpha. Lancer took one hand from the controls and pointed. "At the foot of the cliff on the right!" he shouted over his shoulder.

Scott realized that the land dropped away sharply up ahead, but he couldn't discern just how high they were above the lower terrace. Lancer was cutting their forward speed as they approached the ledge. Scott leaned in to ask him how he planned to negotiate the jump. But all at once Lancer threw his arms straight up and was gone.

Instinctively, Scott grabbed hold of the handlebar controls and saved the mecha from overturning. He looked over his shoulder and saw Lancer squatting on the overhanging branch he had swung himself to, smiling and waving Scott off. Scott was impressed: It had been one heck of a gymnastic feat. But neither of them was in the clear yet. An Invid Trooper broke through the woods and began to open up with disc fire. Lancer executed a Tarzan leap from the tree and disappeared into the undergrowth. Scott lowered his head to the rush of the wind and goosed the cycle. But the cliff face was close now, closer than he had realized, and an instant later he was sailing into blue skies above the treetops. He lost the Cyclone and plummeted on his own, no one to catch him or take note of his alarmed cry. . . .

Elsewhere, Lancer had worked his way back toward the rest of the team. He literally ran into them not a mile from where he had put Scott in charge of the Cyclone. They had three Invid Troopers behind them, devastating the forests with sporadic sprays of fire. Lancer took the point and led them along the same path he and Scott had Cycloned not an hour before. Twilight was giving way to darkness now, and Invid cannon sounds and annihilation discs lent a hellish atmosphere to the scene.

Once again the Troopers succeeded in boxing them in, and once again Rook, Lunk, Annie, and Rand yelled good-byes to one another while explosions rained leaves and forest carpet all over the place. But Scott turned the tide: He had survived his plunge into the trees and made his way to the concealed Veritech. The Invid Pincer ship, as he explained later, was history.

Now the Alpha came tearing into the woods and took out the Trooper whose cannons were ranging in on the team. Then Scott launched the VT straight up into the starry skies, reconfiguring to Battloid at the top of his booster climb and bringing out the mecha's rifle/cannon to deal with his pursuers. Two more Troopers fell to the Alpha's storm, but a third managed to work its way in close enough to inflict a pincer swipe that brought Scott tumbling back to the woods.

The Trooper roared into a long sweeping turn and headed back in on the downed Battloid. Inside, Scott shook himself to clear his head and ran through a rapid assessment of his options as he brought the techno-knight to its feet. The mecha's external pickups brought the team's cries of warning into the cockpit, especially Annie's high-pitched: "Behind you, Scott! Behind you!"

Scott thought the Battloid through a quick about-face in time to see the approaching Trooper. He reached for the launch-tube cover levers. The Invid fired first, blazing discs spinning and twisting out of the cannon muzzles. But Scott's aim was surer: Red-tipped heat-seeking missles ripped from the Battloid's shoulder compartments and homed in on the Invid's dark form, detonating against pincers and torso alike, and giving brief life to a blinding fireball, a brilliant orange midnight sun.

CHAPTER
EIGHT

> *Most commentators overlook the fact that Lancer was a singer long before he was a freedom fighter, and a cross-dresser long before a Yellow Dancer. But he was first and foremost an actor—malleable, dramatic, and narcissistic. And while it's true that he can be linked to certain literary traditions wherein heroes carried out their crusades under the guise of fops and other fabulous fools, Lancer was no Scarlet Pimpernel or comic Zorro: He was a fox of an entirely different order.*

> Zeus Bellow, *The Road to Reflex Point*

PRIOR TO ZOR'S ARRIVAL ON OPTERA, IT WAS THE FLOWer of Life that held the central place in the Invid's naturalistic pantheon. But that was no longer the case. They were aggressive species now every bit as warlike as the Tirolian Masters who defoliated Optera. And they worshipped Protoculture, the bio-energetic by-product Zor had coaxed from the Flowers themselves. They continued to subsist on the Flowers their captive Human population planted and harvested, but it was Protoculture that fueled the army of mecha which kept that enterprise running smoothly and without incident. Indeed, it could be said that the Invid themselves had become more dependent on Zor's discovery than the Robotech Masters ever were.

Enormous amounts of Protoculture were required to oversee and maintain Earth's diverse population centers and to put down uprisings and revolts in the farms and factories. (Exedore would have been chagrinned to learn that the Invid had found their own way to manufacture Protoculture without having to resort to the matrix device that had figured so prominently in the First and Second Robotech Wars.) These reserves, fashioned by Human hands into individual energy canisters suitable for Invid and Terran mecha alike, were stored in scores of warehouses across the globe and guarded by Humans "sympathetic" to the Invid's purpose. The privileges enjoyed by these sympathizers varied; sometimes hostages were taken to assure allegiance, while on other occasions outlaws and petty powerbrokers were given charge. Towns and cities bartered with the Invid overlords for simple freedoms: the right to enjoy a semblance of normal life in exchange for snooping out resistance groups or seeing to it that Protoculture cells did not fall into the wrong hands. Often the Invid allowed those in charge before the invasion to keep their lofty positions, except that there was a new authority to answer to—the Regis and her legions of territorial supervisors who dealt directly with their underlings.

Lancer explained some of this to Scott while the team licked its wounds after their encounter with the Troopers. Even though the episode had consisted largely in their outrunning the Invid, it had nevertheless served to unite the members of the team and instill in each of them a confidence that hadn't been there two days before. They were now beginning to understand and accept each other's strengths and weaknesses, and they were learning to trust one another as well. Without any formal vote or voiced acknowledgment, Scott surfaced as the leader, which was only right given his training and resoluteness. Lunk was something of a sergeant to Scott's lieutenant Annie, everything from den mother to mascot. Rook still held herself separate, but could always be counted on for her instinctive combat sense. And Rand was their backwoods provider, fishing and hunting when he wasn't sitting under a tree scribbling notes to himself. That left only Lancer.

Scott still had misgivings about the man, but as he listened to Lancer's detailed account of the Invid infrastructure and occupation techniques, he began to see him in a new light. The female-singer ploy had yet to be explained, but it was obvious from Lancer's report that the adopted persona of Yellow Dancer had opened many doors to him. He would discuss his former ties with the resistance only in a vague way, but Scott understood that his contacts were as numerous as his information was exhaustive.

The team had retrieved the two other Cyclones from where they had left them in the grass and spent three days in the river gorge dining on pit roasted fish, recuperating, and planning the next move in their northward journey. They were careful about using the mecha now, convinced that Rand's theory was correct. Most of the time the Invid Scouts and Troopers were operating in a kind of background net of Protoculture emanations and couldn't home in on any one source. But when they were engaged in a particular search, their senses were more acute at screening out the random waves from the usually nearby active ones. In any case, it was a moot point at the moment; the Alpha was depleted of charge, and there was scarcely enough left in the Cyclones to power them, let alone reconfigure or fire them.

That's where Norristown entered the picture. Located somewhat east of their present route, it was one of the Southland's largest cities, transplanted like so many others from the devastated north during the reign of Chairman Moran and the formation of the Army of the Southern Cross. The city had prospered throughout and boasted one of the continent's few surviving sports arenas. But most important, it was the site of one of the Invid's Protoculture storage facilities, a heavily fortified castle (constructed years ago in the Hollywood style) that overlooked the city.

Lancer had a map of the place.

And a rather ingenious plan.

Less than a week later, Rook and Annie were on one of the roads leading into Norristown. They made an interesting picture—the blonde in her red and white bodysuit leaning almost casually against the parked Cyclone and Annie in her military greens and ever-present cap perched on the seat like some diminutive ornament. Not five miles away was the city itself, a tight cluster of buildings surrounded by forest, with Drumstick Butte and the hulks of two Zentraedi ships casting their giant shadows from behind. The Protoculture storage facility could be discerned at the foot of the oddly shaped, top-heavy butte, linked to the city below a well-maintained switchbacked roadway.

Rook straightened up at the sound of an approaching vehicle and glanced over at Annie; the youngster nodded and hopped down from the Cyclone's seat to stand alongside her traffic-stopping teammate. Up the road a truck came into view, and Rook threw the driver a playful wink and raised her thumb in a hitchhiker's gesture. Innocently and with well-rehearsed bashfulness, Annie pressed her forefingers together and called for the driver to stop and lend a hand.

The driver halted the truck and climbed down from the cab, taking in a long eyeful of the two marooned girls and their red Cyclone. He bent down to inspect the mecha, complimenting them on the fine condition of the thing, but was sad to report that they were out of Protoculture fuel. This was so common an occurrence that the driver scarcely gave it a second thought; anyone might stumble upon some wonderful specimen of aged Robo-technology only to come to think of it as a worthless piece of junk when the all but irreplaceable Protoculture energy cells were depleted. True, there was a black market, but it was one that few people had access to. Between the needs of the Invid, the resistance, and your everyday 'Culture hounds, Protoculture had become a priceless commodity.

"We were hoping you could fix it," Annie said to the truck driver. "We're on our way to the Yellow Dancer concert in Norristown."

The driver smiled up at her. "Not without Protoculture. There's nothing I can do."

"Hey, mister," Rook said suddenly, as if noticing the driver's Invid-occupation double-C hard-hat emblem for the first time. "You're from the storage facility, aren't you?"

"So?" the man answered, wary now.

"Couldn't you spare us some?" Annie asked, leaning over the Cyclone's seat.

The man snorted. "What're you, nuts, kid? If anyone found out I'd shared my rations, I'd be in deep trouble." He turned his head at the sound of a mechanical click and buzz and found himself staring into the laser muzzle of a strange-looking disc-shaped weapon.

Rook grinned and gestured with the blaster. "Know what? You're *already* in big trouble, buddy. . . ."

Five minutes later the driver had been dragged to the side of the road. His arms and legs were bound with rope, and his mouth was sealed by a piece of wide tape. He continued to struggle while Lunk secured the final knots.

"Relax, buddy," Rook told him. "We're just going to borrow your truck for a while." She hastened off to the spot in the woods where they had moved the vehicle.

Her teammates had the back doors opened. "Well, the first stage went pretty well," Scott was commenting as she walked up.

Rand was leaning against the trailer with his arms crossed. "I had no idea that soldiers also doubled as hijackers, Scott."

Rook looked at both of them impatiently. "Are you guys going to stand here and argue, or are we going to get a move on?"

Scott and Rand exchanged looks. "Let's do it," they said at the same moment.

A short while later the truck roared into town with Lunk at the wheel, the former driver's hard hat and permits now part of his disguise. Rook, Rand, Scott, and Annie were in the rear, but not yet in what would soon be their hiding place. Originally the plan had called for all of them to hide underneath the chassis while the truck was cleared through to the storage facility, but good fortune was on their side in the form of a loft compartment built into the truck's trailer. They could only speculate on what the compartment had been used for, but it was perfectly suited to their present needs. Lunk made one stop along the way to the facility gate—just brief enough to allow Annie to hop out and work her way into the crowds that were already gathering for Yellow Dancer's concert.

"Be sure to make lots of noise," Scott reminded her.

"Come on," she returned, as though insulted. "How do you suppose I got the reputation for being such a loudmouth?"

Scott grinned and began to pull the rear doors closed. He was surprised by the size of the crowds and recalled what Rand had told him earlier: *When people find out Yellow's coming to town, they go completely berserk.* When Annie had jumped out, Scott had glimpsed a poster of the singer pasted to the side of a building: Yellow Dancer in a spaghetti-strapped sundress, some sort of matching turban, low heels, and a pearl collar.

Lancer had left for Norristown three days before the rest of the team. The plan called for him to put a pickup band together and cut a deal with a local promoter, who would secure the sports arena and take care of publicity and logistics. The promoter, a man named Woods, was an old friend of Lancer's and a member of the resistance.

Scott thought back to Lancer's departure—Lancer in his alter-ego guise. Scott couldn't help feeling that Yellow Dancer wasn't just Lancer in female attire but an entirely different personality. Lancer's demeanor changed as well as his voice and carriage. Yellow was a real entity living alongside Lancer in the same body. Scott found it incomprehensible and just a bit unsettling, but it didn't detract from the trust he had in Lancer. Scott was wondering how the second part of Lancer's plan was succeeding when he heard Lunk's fist pounding against the cab of the truck—the signal for Scott, Rand, and Rook to take to the overhead compartment. That meant the truck was nearing the twin-towered security gate on the road below the storage facility.

Farther along the road that wound up toward the base of Drumstick Butte was the barracks of the security force that staffed and guarded the storage facility. The chief of station, Colonel Briggs, was a large, beefy man with salt-and-pepper hair and a thick mustache. He was in his office in the barracks, feet up on the desk, daydreaming over a color photo of Yellow Dancer that had appeared in the morning edition of the city's newspaper when one of his staff arrived with good news.

"We've been asked to supply security at Yellow Dancer's concert this afternoon," the staffer reported. He wore a blue-gray uniform with a red upturned collar, similar in cut and design to that worn by the colonel. A single red star adorned the front of his brimmed cap. The Invid had made a point of allowing local customs and garb to remain unchanged in Norristown and numerous other strongholds throughout the Southlands. "Shall I refuse the request, sir?" the staffer wanted to know.

Briggs didn't bother to lower the newspaper, which effectively concealed him from the staffer. He hummed to himself, finishing up his fanciful daydream scenario before replying. "Are you out of your mind?" he said at last. "If something should happen to Yellow Dancer, it's *our* reputation that will suffer. Send every available man down to the arena."

"But sir," the staffer pointed out haltingly, "we can't risk leaving the facility unguarded. . . ."

"Nonsense," the colonel said from behind his paper. "What time is the concert scheduled to end?"

"Around three-thirty, but—"

"And what time are the Intercessors arriving to pick up the shipment?"

"Four o'clock, but—"

"Then there's no problem." Briggs set the paper aside, got up from behind the desk, and walked over to the office window. "What can happen?" he said, gesturing to the facility half a mile away at the top of the switchbacked access road. "The facility's impregnable . . . And besides, I'd like to oversee Yellow Dancer's security *personally*." He swung around to his lieutenant. "See to it that she expects me."

Rumor had it that the storage facility was originally a castle imported stone by stone from Europe during the mid-1800s by a renegade nobleman from Transylvania. It saw more than one hundred years of alteration and modernization before being substantially renovated (in the Hollywood style) by a sports event promoter who fell heir to the place in 2015. Much of Norristown, including the arena, owed its existence to the same man.

The building, with its mansard roof and numerous spires, still retained a Provençal look, but this was overshadowed by the fantastical elements added on during the last twenty-five years, primarily the east wing's crenellated tower. Three-quarters of a mile down the road was the twin-towered main gate, where Lunk and the others were presently stopped.

"I'm here to run a check on the cooling systems," Lunk said to the helmeted guard who approached the driver's side window.

"Your permit," the guard said nastily.

Lunk handed the papers down for the man to read, while a second guard moved to the back of the truck to have a look inside. "It's clean, Fred!" Lunk heard the man call out a minute later. The guard perused the permit a while longer, then returned it. "You'd better be clean on the way out, too," he warned Lunk. Lunk saw sentries at the other tower frisking a white-coveralled driver.

"You got it," he told the guard.

The guard waved him through and opened the fence that spanned the roadway. Lunk threw the truck into gear and drove off, removing his hat and wiping away the sweat that had collected on his forehead. Two trucks filled with security personnel passed him going in the opposite direction, a sign that Lancer's request might have been granted. At the top of the switchbacks, Lunk backed the truck toward the shipping entrance. There were only three or four guards on patrol, and not one of them even glanced at Lunk while he climbed down from the cab and threw open the rear doors.

"We're in, gang," he said loudly enough for his friends to hear.

Rook, Rand, and Scott lowered themselves from the loft compartment and entered the facility. Scott unfolded Lancer's map and checked it against their location. "This one," he told Rook and Rand, indicating an air duct grate along one wall. Lunk helped them move several crates over to the wall. Scott climbed up first, rechecked the map, and peered through the grate. Satisfied, he nodded, and Rook and Rand joined him. The two men went to work on the bolts that held the grating to its frame, and in a moment they were able to lift the panel free. Scott and Rand crawled in. Lunk handed rope, a tool pouch, and an aluminum carry case up to Rook. She waved him good luck and followed Scott's lead into the horizontal duct.

Less than fifteen feet into the duct, Scott stopped and whispered: "The control room is on the third floor. It should take us about ten minutes to get there."

Rook could barely discern him in the darkness. Ten minutes was going to feel like an eternity.

Down below, the arena was rapidly filling to capacity and Annie was circulating in front of the stage doing what she did best: inciting the crowd.

"... At her last concert a whole bunch of people got up on stage, and everybody started partying and having a good ole time," she told everyone within earshot. "Some of us even got to go backstage with Yellow Dancer after the concert and party some more! But this one's going to be the best! I hear that she might not perform like this again, so we better make this the one to remember. Right?!"

"All right!" several people shouted. "Party time!"

Meanwhile, Yellow Dancer was entertaining guests in her backstage dressing room. She had changed to a sleeveless pink and burgundy pants outfit with a matching bowed headband, which held her hair up and off her neck.

"At the last concert, some of my fans came up on stage and really made a mess of things," she was explaining, facing the mirror while she applied eye liner. "I'd rather that didn't happen again."

"We won't allow that here," Briggs, the facility security chief, said from behind her. Yellow smiled at him in the mirror. "We'll do our job and guarantee you complete security. As long as nothing happens to bring the Invid down on us."

"Those horrible creatures," Yellow said, twisting up her face.

"Aah, they're not so bad once you get to know them," the chief started to say.

Lancer's friend, Woods, threw him a conspiratorial wink from a corner of the room. He was a handsome young man with a pencil-thin mustache whose taste ran to calfskin jackets and black leather ties. Just now he was holding the large bouquet of flowers Briggs had brought along for Yellow Dancer. "We know you'll do your best, Colonel," Woods said encouragingly.

Lancer saw the chief's puffy face turn red with embarrassment. "You're damn right we will."

"And I want to thank you *so* much for the flowers," Yellow gushed, turning away from the mirror now to flash Briggs a painted smile. "They're lovely."

Briggs leered at her. "Anything for you, Yellow, anything you want."

Scott, Rook, and Rand had reached the third floor of the facility. The duct opened out into a small area that served as the relay center for the facility's security systems. Scott and Rand moved in to try to make sense of the tangle of wires and switches that covered two full walls of the room. It took several minutes to locate the feeds from the security cameras, but the rest was child's play. Rook unsnapped the clasps on the carry case and began to hand over the devices Lunk assured them would scramble the a/v signals. Scott and Rand quickly attached these to the feeder cables and set off on the next leg of their cramped journey.

The map called for a brief return to the air duct system before they could enter the actual storage area. But once through this, they would be free to move about at will—assuming Lunk's devices did the trick. They dropped out of the duct into a maintenance corridor that encircled the supply room but had no access to it except for a single elbow conduit located clear around the back of the building. Rand volunteered to test the effectiveness of Lunk's scramblers by making faces at one of the surveillance cameras. When no sirens went off and no guards came running, the trio figured they were in the clear and decided to use one of the maintenance carts to convey them to the conduit—an open-topped electric affair with two seats and a single headlamp that brought them around back in a quarter the time it would have taken them to walk.

They stopped at the first elbow conduit and commenced a careful count. Rook looked over the map, while Scott took charge of noting their position relative to the first main.

"Under the main line, thirteenth from the right," Scott said, recalling the scrawled notation on the map. He gestured to an elbow up ahead. "That must be it."

The conduit was made of light-gauge metal; it was a good four feet in circumference and stood at least six feet high from floor to right-angle bend. It was held in place by a circular flange, but promised to be flexible enough once the bolts securing the flange to the floor were undone. Rand and Scott took box wrenches from the tool pouch and immediately set to work. At the same time, Rook took a coil of rope from the cart and began to tie it fast to one of the adjacent elbows.

When the last of the bolts had been loosened and removed, Rook and Scott shoved the conduit to one side and bent down to peer into the shaft below.

Rand squinted and smiled to himself as his eyes fixed upon the objects of their search: crate after crate of Protoculture canisters, each the size and shape of a squat thermos.

"There's a mountain of it down here," he reported.

Scott gave a tug on the rope Rook had tied to the conduit. "Feels strong enough," he commented while Rook tied the other end around her waist. "The security system down there is still operative. You touch anything—the wall, the ceiling, the floor—and you'll trigger it."

Rook sat down and let her legs dangle through the opening. Rand and Scott took hold of the rope and signaled their readiness. "All right," she told them. "Let's get this over with before I change my mind."

Yellow Dancer's concert was under way. She streaked onto the stage like a comet, with the band already laying down the intro to "Look Up!" and the audience of several thousand roaring their appreciation. It was a heavy-message number that had become something of an anthem in the Southlands, and Yellow loved singing it. She stood with her legs spread apart, one hand on her hip, holding the mike like an upturned glass, her body accenting the beat.

Another winter's day
Another gray reminder that what used to be
Has gone away.
It's really hard to say,
How long we'll have to live with our insanity;
We have to pay for all we use,
We never think before we light the fuse . . .
Look up, look up, look up!
The sky is fall-ing!
Look up,
There's something up you have to know.
Before you try to go outside,
To take in the view,
Look up, because the sky
Could fall on you . . .

Yellow looked to the stage wings, where the colonel was eagerly trying to stomp his foot to the music, an ear-to-ear grin on his face, his men vigilant throughout the arena.

Loaded down with canisters of Protoculture fished from the storage room, the electric cart sped away from the maintenance corridor and entered a stone serviceway, damp, foul-smelling, and seemingly unused for centuries. Rook, still dizzy from her upside-down descent into the storage room, had the map spread open in her lap while Scott drove. In the dim ambient light, she tried to match juncture points in the serviceway with the vague scrawls indicated on the map. Finally she told Scott to stop the cart. He got out and began to inspect the stones at eye level along the right-hand wall of the corridor.

"Should be over here somewhere," Rook heard him say. She watched him lay his hand against one of the stones, and in a moment the wall was opening. Another corridor was revealed, perpendicular to the first and decidedly downhill.

"And this is supposed to lead to the concert hall?" Rook said uncertainly.

"Looks to me like it leads to the dungeon," Rand said behind her.

Back at the wheel, Scott edged the cart forward into the dark passageway. "Lancer said it was an escape route constructed by the man who originally had this place built."

"Well, let's hope so," Rook answered him as the stone wall reassembled itself behind them.

The ramp dropped at a steep angle that sorely tested the electric cart's brakes, but the important thing was that they were leaving the facility behind.

Rand was encouraged. According to his own calculations the passageway was indeed leading them in the direction of the arena. "Piece of cake," he said from his uncomfortable position atop the Protoculture canisters stacked in the bed of the cart. "We should have taken more while we had the chance."

"Don't be so smart," Scott said stiffly. "We're not out of here yet."

Rand leaned forward between the front seats. "What's there to worry about now? The concert's on, we've got the 'Culture, Lunk'll be waiting for us with open arms..."

"Mr. Confidence all of a sudden," Rook snorted from the shotgun seat. Scott was easing up on the brakes, and the cart was traveling along at a good clip now. Rook was holding her hair in place with one hand when the cart's headlamp revealed a solid wall blocking their exit.

"Hold on!" Scott yelled, pulling up on the hand brake.

The rear end of the cart bounced and swerved as the brakes locked, but Scott managed to remain in control and brought the vehicle to a halt with room to spare. The trio regarded the wall and began to wonder whether they might have missed a turnoff earlier on.

"I didn't see any side tunnels," said Scott. "And according to Lancer's map there's only supposed to be this one passageway."

"The map's been accurate up to now," Rook added, running her fingers through her tangled hair. "Where'd we go wrong?"

"Maybe we have to give the wall a push or something, like up top," Rand suggested.

Scott was just about to step out and have a look, when he heard a deep rumbling sound behind him. The trio turned to watch helplessly as a massive stone partition dropped from the tunnel's ceiling.

"Now what?" Scott said after a moment.

"They must be on to us somehow!" Rook said. But Scott disagreed. "Those a/v scramblers still have fifteen minutes of life left in them. I think we must have—"

Scott cut himself off as a new sound began to infiltrate their silent tomb. It began with a grating sound of stone moving against stone, then softened to a sibilance before gushing loud and clear.

"Water!" Rand yelled. "We're being flooded!"

CHAPTER
NINE

It was just a case of overcompensation again: We went from having no plan to too much plan!

Rand, *Notes on the Run*

YELLOW DANCER PRANCED ACROSS THE STAGE, pointing and gesturing to the crowd, swinging the microphone over her head as though it were a lariat. She was in the midst of a hard driving number now, a flat-out rocker that had the audience dancing in the aisles and pressing forward toward the stage.

Annie was helping this along.

"Let's get this party under way!" she shouted from her cramped space near the front. "Let's get up on stage!"

Yellow spied Annie in the crowd and smiled while she sang. She threw herself into an impromptu spin, shaking her hips and urging the band to kick up the volume somewhat. She turned again and launched herself across the stage in a kind of Jagger strut, inching her way toward the edge with each pass and beckoning the fans to join her.

Woods and the colonel looked on from the wings.

"What an incredible performer," Briggs was saying. Woods noticed the glint in the colonel's eye as he watched Yellow twirl herself like some sort of singing acrobat. "She's amazing...And these kids look like they're ready to jump out of their socks."

The man is practically drooling. Woods laughed to himself. "They are beginning to get a bit out of hand," he told Briggs, a forced note of concern in his voice. He motioned to the front ranks of the audience, where the crowds were pushing hard against the security force's arm-link cordon. "Don't you think it would be wise to keep a van ready out back just in case we have to get Yellow Dancer out of here in a hurry?"

Woods saw Briggs blanch. He called out to one of the men guarding the stage entrance and told him bring a van to the rear door, while Woods suppressed a smile and turned to watch Yellow strut her stuff.

On the cold stone floor of a small, seldom-used room beneath the stage, Lunk sat cross-legged, blowing up balloons. Several hundred of these helium-filled colored globes had already been inflated and secreted in a compartment behind the bandshell itself, but the ones Lunk was busy preparing had to serve a special purpose. To each grouping of four balloons, Lunk added a carefully concealed propellant device in addition to a sensor that would allow the four-color group to home in on a prearranged beacon signal transmitted from the outskirts of Norristown, close to the spot where the team had left the Cyclones and the Veritech.

When Lunk had filled the last of the balloons, he crawled over and shut down the helium tanks, only then realizing how spaced out he was from inhaling the gas.

He glanced at the room's brick rear wall and moved over to it now, running his hands over the stones and searching for any signs of the doorway indicated on Lancer's map of the facility and linking passageway. But he could find no evidence of seams or fractures in the mortar. Perhaps it could be opened only from inside the tunnel, he thought, checking his watch. He would know soon enough, in any case. . . .

The cart turned out to be watertight. Not that this would have been some wondrous piece of news under normal circumstances, but given the tunnel trio's present condition it was one of those small miracles to be thankful for. It meant that they were able to remain seated while the water rose around them rather than have to exhaust themselves trying to remain afloat in water that was well over their heads. Of course, this, too, seemed a minor consolation.

A few four-pack canisters of Protoculture were bobbing about in the cold water, and Rand was sitting on the front bumper of the cart looking like the world was about to end.

Which was certainly an appropriate enough response, seeing how the water was still pouring into their tomb with no signs of letting up, and the cold ceiling was only four feet above them now. But Rook, who seldom had a good word to say about anything, was trying to cheer Rand up.

"C'mon, pal, try not to get so down in the dumps."

Rand stared at her in disbelief. "Down in the dumps?" he said, gesturing to the room, their situation. "What d'ya think, I should be happy about getting a chance to wash up before I die?"

"It's my fault," Scott told them. "I should have considered the possibility that some of the older defensive systems would still be operational."

Rook shook her head. "Don't blame yourself, Scott."

"Let 'im," Rand argued. "Why not? He got us into this, didn't he?"

"*We* got us into this," Rook said, raising her voice.

Scott told them both to shut up. "Besides, we might get a lucky break yet."

Rand and Rook waited for an explanation.

"If the a/v scramblers fade before the water gets much higher, we'll probably get to face a firing squad instead of drowning."

In the stage wings, the colonel looked out at Yellow's screaming audience and swung harshly to Woods. "If this mob gets any more unruly, the Invid are to going to send a few Troopers in here and we'll have all hell to pay!"

Woods had to agree. Yellow was supposed to have finished up already, but instead she was going into yet another encore. The crowds were whipped up into such a frenzy that the arena seemed unable to contain it.

Yellow Dancer sensed Woods's concern and turned to him briefly as she gyrated around the stage. *Where is Scott?* she asked herself as the band revved up. She took several giant steps toward the wings and tried to flash her accomplice a signal, touching her earring and shaking her head as if to indicate that she hadn't heard from Lunk yet.

Woods acknowledged his understanding with a shrug and a slight gesture toward the chief, who was pacing in the wings like a nervous animal.

Yellow brought the mike up and asked if everyone was all right, holding the mike out to them as they screamed replies. Again they strained at the security cordon, and several kids succeeded in making it onto the stage before being scooped up by guards and carried off. Something had to be done *quickly*!

* * *

Scott, Rook, and Rand had scarcely a foot of breathing space left, and the water level was still rising. Things had reached the desperate stage a few minutes before, and now the three of them were in the water pushing up against each and every ceiling stone, praying that one would give.

"That story about the hero escaping through a loose stone is just a fairy tale," Rand was saying, when his hands felt the stone budge. For a moment he was speechless, but finally he managed to gulp out the words: "It moved! The stone moved!"

"She's *already* gone a half hour overtime!" the chief shouted to Woods. "I want the concert wrapped up—and I mean *now*!"

"But look at the kids," Woods tried. "They're having the time of their lives. I mean, after all, when do they ever get a chance to let off a little—"

"Now!" the chief said firmly. "Or this will be the last chance they ever get. Do you understand me?"

Woods backed away and threw a signal to the control booth: They were to cut the power as soon as Yellow finished her song. . . .

Lunk, meanwhile, was pacing back and forth in the small area beneath the stage. Scott was way overdue. There were no contingency plans other than to get out of Norristown as quickly as possible. Annie and Lancer would be all right, but Lunk could be identified by the guards at the facility tower. But just as he was resigning himself to this, he heard sounds of movement behind him. He swung around in time to see his waterlogged friends step through the parted wall. Each of them was toting Protoculture canister packs.

"Well, it's about time," Lunk said to them, eyeing

their soaked clothing. "What happened to you guys—you come by way of the river, or what?"

"We'll explain later," Scott said hurriedly, already fastening the packs to the balloon clusters. "Signal Lancer, and let's get this show on the road."

Yellow was aware that the control room and sound personnel had been ordered to cut the power, so she was milking the final song for all it was worth, extending the chorus and encouraging the audience to join in, in the hopes that Scott would appear in time. But by now she had done all she could; the band was finishing up with an interminable one-chord wrap-up, and she was just about to make the grand leap that would cut it off. Then she heard a small but unmistakable flashing tone emitted by her left earring. It was Lunk's signal: *Scott had made it!*

"Thank you! Thank you, all of you!" Yellow yelled into the microphone over deafening applause. Yellow gestured to Annie and watched as she began to worm her way toward the cordon, readying the pass that would admit her backstage.

People in the crowd were pointing to something in the air now, and Annie got a glimpse of a skyful of balloons before she disappeared through the door to the stage wings.

"I love you!" Yellow added as she left the stage.

The plan called for Scott, Rook, and Rand to infiltrate themselves among Yellow Dancer's retinue of sidemen and bodyguards, all of whom had been handpicked by Woods. At the same time, Lunk's role was to see to it that the waiting police van was rendered safe and secure.

This was easily accomplished, thanks to the fact that the guard was napping when Lunk stole up to the driver's side door. Lunk pummeled the man into a more lasting sleep. Scott, Rook, and Rand took to the canvas-backed van, while Lunk dragged the guard off to one side and began to change into the man's police helmet, shirt, and trousers. Annie appeared a moment later, followed by Yellow, who was clutching two wardrobe suitcases under her arms. The colonel was inside the arena, waiting patiently at Yellow's dressing-room door for the singer to arrive. Woods's team, meanwhile, had spirited her out a rear entry and was now doing its best to keep things backstage suitably chaotic.

"So, you're alive after all," Yellow said breathlessly, running to the truck and passing her valises up to Scott.

"Never underestimate the best," Rand said, full of importance.

Yellow gave Rand the once-over and smiled bemusedly. "Why are you so wet?"

"Come on, get in," Rook broke in. "It'll be your bedtime story."

Yellow climbed up into the back of the truck, already pulling off the clothes that separated her from Lancer. Rand threw himself in and unfurled the rear canvas drape. Annie ran around to the passenger seat and settled herself, while a smiling Lunk did the same behind the wheel. He knew how ridiculous he looked in the smaller man's uniform and helmet and couldn't keep from laughing.

A moment later the truck was screeching away from the stage entrance, just short of a crowd of fans who had found their way back there. Woods stood pleased in the doorway, silently wishing Yellow and her friends a smooth getaway.

Back outside the dressing-room door, Colonel Briggs was glancing impatiently at his watch and complaining under his breath about how much time women required to change outfits. He contemplated walking in on Yellow, wondering if he would be able to catch her at a vulnerable moment. The thought was blossoming into a Technicolor fantasy when one of his guards ran up to him and saluted.

"There's been a break-in at the facility," the staffer reported in a rush. "Thirty-eight cases of Protoculture are missing."

The colonel's mouth fell open. "B-but . . . *how*?"

"They used some kind of scramblers to disrupt the surveillance cameras and apparently lowered themselves into the storage room from one of the overhead maintenance corridors."

Briggs grabbed the man by the lapels and pulled him close. "How could they get through the towers? Were all vehicles searched?"

"Yes, chief, everyone was searched," the man managed to get out. "They must have found another way out."

The colonel shook the man, took a few steps, then whirled on him again. "Search the city! Set up roadblocks! I want them found—*alive*!"

The staffer saluted. "We'll do what we can. But most of our units are still working crowd control outside."

"Forget the crowds!" Briggs barked. "Get every man on it."

The city's streets were soon filled with police vans —sirens hooting, tearing around corners in search of a team of sneak thieves. But by this time, Lunk was edging the van out of town, way ahead of the roadblocks the colonel's currently understaffed security force were attempting to set up at all possible points of egress.

The colonel's own van screeched to a halt in a cobblestone square, where it rendezvoused with three others that were returning from various checkpoints. Briggs leapt out and approached one of his lieutenants, demanding all pertinent information.

"And don't tell me they've disappeared," he warned the already shaking staffer.

"We have reason to believe that they made their getaway in a police van," the lieutenant updated. "So we're in the process of having our men check each van they come across to ascertain the identity of those inside."

"Good," the colonel said haltingly. Then: "You mean to tell me that your men are out there *searching each other*?!" He was about to say more, when he heard a small crash behind him, as if something had fallen from a rooftop. Turning, Briggs saw a cluster of red, yellow, and green balloons weighted down by something he couldn't make out until he had taken three steps toward it.

"Protoculture canisters!" he exclaimed, kneeling beside the helium balloons and their precious cargo. He looked up and saw scores more drifting high over the city on a northeast wind. "Gather up all those balloons," he ordered the lieutenant. "Shoot them down if you have to!... And bring me that *singer*," he hastened to add, thinking back to the concert and its colorful finale...

Briggs was hurrying back to his van when a vehicle from the facility pulled alongside him.

"Have you found them?" he asked eagerly.

"No," the driver answered. "But the Invid Intercessors have arrived at the facility... And they wanna speak to you...."

The getaway truck and the rigged balloon clusters arrived at the transmitter site at the same time, a clearing in the woods that fringed the northeastern outskirts of

Norristown. The team hopped out and began gathering up the canisters. Rook and Lancer were heading for the Cyclones when they heard Annie yell and saw her point to the sky.

"Invid!"

There were five Troopers, coming in fast from the southwest but still several miles off. Scott told everyone to grab whatever canister packs they could carry and run for the mecha. Lancer, already suited up in battle armor, headed directly for one of the Cyclones and inserted a fresh canister into the cylinderlike fuel cell below the mecha's engine. He straddled the cycle and activated the ignition, watching with delight as the power displays came to life, glowing with an unprecedented brightness. Nearby, Scott was in the cockpit of the Veritech, Lunk attending to the refueling.

Rook was preparing to power up her red Cyclone when she saw Lancer lift off and reconfigure to Battle Armor mode. Beside her, Rand was strapping on the last of his Cyclone armor.

"Rand, did you remember to put in a fresh canister?" she asked him, certain he had forgotten.

"Oh, right," he returned, and stooped to insert the fresh pack.

"Dimwit," Rook scolded him as she roared off, going to Battle Armor mode a moment later. Rand followed her up and through to reconfiguration, and the two of them streaked off to assist Lancer, who was going head to head with two Invid Troopers.

Lancer had coaxed the Troopers to the ground and was executing leaps to avoid pincer swipes. Frustrated now, one of the creatures was ready to bring its shoulder cannons into play.

Lancer stepped back when he saw the muzzles begin to glow; Rook and Rand had set down behind him, and the three of them felt the blast of the first charge.

"Let's not push our luck until the Alpha arrives," Lancer said over the Cyclone's tactical net.

The two Troopers took to the air, then swooped down for strafing runs. But Rand had tailed one of them and launched shoulder-tubed Scorpions before the Invid could fire. The Trooper took two missiles to the face and went down, leaking a thick green fluid.

Rook took out a second creature; Lancer dispatched a third that was giving Rand a hard time, bringing the odds more to everyone's liking by the time Scott got the Veritech up.

The two remaining Troopers kept to the ground, dishing out annihilation discs against the incoming Alpha, but Scott flew undaunted into the fire, loosing the VT's own brand of vengeful energy. With a last-minute leap, one of the Invid narrowly escaped the Alpha's angry red-tipped missiles, but the second stood its ground and suffered for it.

Scott continued his power dive against the fifth and final Invid now; it had put down again, emptying its up-turned cannons against him. Scott dropped through the annihilation discs like some sort of slalom flyer, getting off one shot before pulling out of his dive. But that one connected, impacting the Trooper's midsection and splitting it in half.

Scott banked hard at the top of his climb and fell away toward Norristown and the enormous buttes which over-shadowed the city. Down below he could discern a long line of police vehicles speeding from the city toward the team's somewhat ravaged forest clearing.

Hearing Scott's warning over the tac net, Rand, Rook, and Lancer landed their mecha and reconfigured to Cyclone mode. Annie and Lunk were running around gathering up late-arrival balloonloads of Protoculture canisters. They took to the police van at Scott's amplified insistence and sped off following the Cyclones' lead, the setting sun huge and blood-red at their backs.

CHAPTER
TEN

Rook's hometown [Trenchtown, formerly Cavern City] typified an offbeat trend in city planning that was popular between the [First and Second Robotech] Wars. This plan, called the Obscuro Movement, was formed as a reaction to threats of invasion, real and imaginary, by Zentraedi, Tirolian Masters, Invid, or any of a number of self-styled conquerors and terrestrial invaders. Cities were constructed in the most unlikely places—on the tops of mesas, the bottom of ravines, the heart of darkness—anywhere deemed unassailable by founders and would-be leaders.

"Southlands," *History of the Third Robotech War*, Vol. XXII

RAND'S JOURNAL PICKS UP THE STORY:

"We had a good enough jump on Norristown's police force to lose them without too much hassle. But just to make sure, Scott saw to it that our escape route was wiped out behind us with a few well-placed missiles from the Alpha. Chances are that most of the vans turned tail as soon as they caught sight of the Veritech anyway. We could only guess what the Invid decided to extract in the way of retribution; at the very least some heads were going to roll.

"We were all feeling great. The Cyclones practically had to be reigned in, thanks to the fresh infusion of 'Culture. Scott thought that the Invid-manufactured batch was more powerful than the 'Culture Earth mecha had been operating on during the last twenty years. The only thing that held us back was the police van we had commandeered. But it seemed a wiser idea to accept the thing's limitations rather than carry Lunk and Annie on the Cyclones or in the fighter. It continued to puzzle us why the Invid didn't simply overwhelm us with Troopers; with three Cycs running at high speed, it should have been easy enough to track us down. But Scott explained that they had demonstrated the same sort of tactical shortcomings in previous encounters. I was always trying to press him to elaborate, but he was reticent to talk about Tirol and the other worlds he had seen.

"We traveled north for two days almost without letup, using the scrip Woods had given Lancer to barter supplies and bedrolls in some of the settlements we passed through. The terrain was arid and rugged, characterized by buttes and tors and mesas similar to those around Norristown but softened by small skyblue lakes and patches of hardwood forest. We made our first real camp alongside one of these cold water lakes. We had come across a dozen wild cattle earlier on and shot one for provisions, so we were eating well and getting good rest in the sleeping bags. Scott ran us through a kind of mutual-appreciation debriefing on the Norristown raid. More and more we were beginning to feel like an actual team and not just six individuals on the run.

"I tried to insist that we make camp in the woods, but everyone else was intent on enjoying the sunlight at the edge of the lake. I put Annie in charge of gathering firewood, and she kept coming in with nearly petrified pieces of hardwood. (Not that we really even needed the fire—I was doing most of the cooking over a propane stove anyway—but a fire was their idea of camping out, and I wasn't into spoiling anyone's fun.) Lunk whittled when he wasn't going over the Cyclone and VT systems. Scott cleaned and maintained the ordnance. Lancer was finding it easier and easier to relax around us, and he would often fall quite naturally into a kind of midway mode that was part Lancer the freedom fighter and part Yellow Dancer. He had fashioned a shower for himself by punching a series of holes in one of our old cook pots. He would bring in water heated on the fire and pour this into the holed pot he had fastened to an overhead branch. Lunk got a big charge out of this and once tried to interrupt Lancer while he was showering. It was a pretty comical exchange that ended with Lancer calling Lunk "a mindless brute," and Lunk amazed that Lancer of all people should be modest.

"Rook was the only one keeping to herself. I would see her standing alone by the lake, absently skimming stones across the surface. It was obvious that she had something disturbing on her mind, but she didn't want to share it with the rest of us. Scott also sensed it. I have since learned what the brooding was all about, but back then all I could sense was Rook's uneasiness and an inexplicable feeling of helplessness. The only time the team discussed it was after she had turned on Annie, who was only trying to entice her to join us around the fire.

"'What d'ya think's wrong with her?' Lunk asked the rest of us.

"'Women's mood changes are unpredictable,' Lancer said knowledgeably in Yellow's voice. He had just stepped from the shower and was wearing a long yellow terry robe and had his hair up under a towel wrapped turban-style around his head.

"'Just leave her alone,' I suggested. 'She'll come out of it.' But Scott took issue with me.

"'No. This is different.'

"'Let it go,' I started to say, but Scott was already on his feet and off to seek her out. I felt compelled to tag along at a discreet distance, probably because I was afraid of Scott's scoring points where I couldn't.

"Rook was standing near the lake. She didn't even respond when Scott called her; I saw him give a small shrug and pull out that holo-locket he wore around his neck—the one Marlene gave him shortly before she went down with her ship. I wasn't sure just what he was thinking, but what bothered me most was the idea that Rook's moodiness was going to have a contagious effect on the team.

"In a moment, however, we all had bigger problems to deal with.

"I saw Scott and Rook turn at the same moment to stare at something off in the distance, so I stepped out from cover to see what was going on and heard the telltale approach of an Invid ship even before I saw the thing appear from behind one of the buttes. It was a large patrol ship, a rust-brown number boasting twice the firepower of a Trooper. I ran back to the fire and started stomping it out, while Scott and the others headed for the woods. The Invids hadn't spotted us, and it wasn't likely that a simple campfire was going to bring it down, but for all we knew the patrol ships had now been ordered to incinerate anything that moved. Rook's Cyclone was my main concern; she had thoughtlessly left it by the lake in plain view.

"The patrol ship swept along the shore directly over our smoldering campfire and headed out toward the lake, but suddenly it swung about, its optic sensor scanning the woods. I voiced a silent prayer that the thing wouldn't spot us, and what seemed an eternity later, the Invid blasted up and away from our small piece of tranquillity.

"'Close one,' I said when the thing had disappeared. 'But it looks like we're safe for the moment.'

"'Uh uh,' Scott said worriedly, shaking his head.

'We've got to assume they found us.' He saw the chagrined looked on my face and hastened to add: 'It might have gone for reinforcements—we'd be foolish to remain here any longer.'

"Lunk was taking stock of our surroundings. 'Bad place to get caught if they mean business. I'm for splitting.'

"'Then let's move it,' Scott said.

"I knelt down by the remains of our fire and poked at the coals. 'So much for dinner...'

"Lancer sauntered by me, dangling an outstretched limp wrist from the robe's broad sleeve and feigning a bored yawn. 'Well, it didn't look very appetizing anyway,' he minced.

"Movement was likely to make matters worse, but there was high ground nearby that provided substantially more in the way of cover. We rode out most of the afternoon looking over our shoulders and waiting for Scott's warnings over the tac net, but no Invid appeared. It was beginning to look as though we hadn't been seen after all, but no one was making an issue of having abandoned our campsite. The air in the highlands was invigorating, and we found an expanse of conifer forest to call home for the night. Even Lancer had to admit that the steaks were tasty, and Rook, who had been sullen and lone-riding all day, seemed to be coming around some.

"I woke up sometime during the night and noticed that Rook wasn't in her bag. I took a quick look around, counting heads and quickly realizing that Scott had the watch. (Actually, it turned out that he wasn't on watch at all, but I imagined him absent, once again falling victim to a kind of irrational jealousy.) I unzippered myself from the bag, egged on by thoughts of Rook and Scott cozying it up somewhere in the woods. *Just lean on my shoulder and tell me all about it, Rook,* I could almost hear Scott saying, when it was *my* shoulder she should have been leaning on!

"The moon was full and low in the west, casting long shadows across ground cushioned with pine needles. To a sound track of insect songs, I stole silently through the trees and spied Rook, alone, in a clearing dominated by a tall oak. Her Cyclone was parked nearby; obviously she had wheeled it away from the pack while the rest of us slept. She seemed to be staring transfixed at something carved into the trunk, but I was too far back to make out what it was.

"I heard her say, 'Why—why did it happen?' and the next thing I knew she was hopping onto the Cyclone and moving off. I ran after her and thought about calling her. The word or name *ROMY* was carved into the tree trunk. It didn't mean anything to me, but it had obviously touched off something in Rook. I went back for my Cyclone and pushed it a good hundred yards from the woods before starting it up and going after her.

"It wasn't hard to follow her trail, and there was enough ambient moonlight for me to tail her without bringing up the Cyclone's headlamp. Straight off, it was apparent that she knew where she was going: She cut through the woods in the direction of the main road, headed north for several miles, then turned east along a rutted track that coursed over a barren, seemingly endless stretch of land. She was perhaps a half a mile ahead of me when I saw her suddenly veer off sharply to the right for no apparent reason. Fortunately, I thought to cut my speed some, because just short of the spot where she had made her turn I realized that the land dropped steeply away. I braked and threw the Cyclone into a sharp turn that brought me close to the edge of a narrow chasm, scarcely the width of a city block. In the darkness below I could discern two rows of ruined buildings backed against the canyon's walls, almost as tall as the chasm was deep and facing each other across a single potholed street. Still a good distance ahead of me, Rook was disappearing into a kind of open-faced bunker that projected from the land as though it were a natural outcropping. Nearby were the tops of two massive circular shafts I guessed were exhaust ports for the city below.

"I twisted the Cyclone's throttle and accelerated into the unlit tunnel, not knowing what to expect."

"The city was dark and deserted-looking, claustrophobic due to the closeness of the canyon walls but threatening in a way that had nothing to do with the uniqueness of its location. Rook was still unaware of my presence. She had parked her Cyclone halfway along the street, dismounted, and was now peering into the permaplas window of a lighted and apparently occupied ground-floor apartment. I think I came close to abandoning my little game just then; the sight of Rook eavesdropping on someone called into question my own position. But I decided to hang in, rationalizing that I was simply keeping an eye out in case anyone came wandering in on Rook's scene. Again, I was too far away to make out exactly what was going on: I heard Rook say, 'Romy,' as a man in a yellow shirt passed by the window. That at least explained the tree trunk carving and Rook's knowledge of the area. She had been here before; perhaps was native to the place. A moment later I heard Rook's sharp intake of breath. She had turned away from the window as if in disbelief.

"'My sister Lilly?' she asked softly.

"Rook took a few backward steps, straddled the Cyclone, and roared off. I stomped my mecha into gear and followed. I had all intentions of catching up to her now and having a heart-to-heart, but suddenly there were three more vehicles in the street, tearing out in front of Rook from an alleyway that ended at the canyon wall. They were solid-hubbed Harley choppers with twin front headlights, dressed down for rough and ready street riding. The riders were of the same ilk—Mohawked, shaved-skulled, maniacal. They were chasing down two young women, taunting, gesturing, and otherwise cat-and-mousing them. I saw the Mohawked rider come alongside and douse them with beer from the bottle he was carrying. Then, when one of the women fell—a cute brunette in knee boots and a full skirt—the riders began to circle her, revving their bikes and promising a wide variety of injustices. The only helmeted rider had taken hold of the second woman and was grabbing what he could, heedless of the fury of her fists.

"Rook, meanwhile, had edged her bike up to the perimeter of the riders' circle; now, as they were making grabs for the downed girl, she switched on the Cyclone's headlight and brought it to bear on the group. Stunned, the riders brought hands up to shield their eyes.

"'You Snakes haven't changed a bit,' Rook growled. She turned the front wheel aside so the bikers could get a look at the hand blaster she had trained on them. 'Well, now don't tell me you've forgotten my face . . .'

"The Mohawked rider, who I now noticed had a blue heart tattooed on his left arm, squinted and scowled. 'Why, it's Rook!'

"The two women broke free of their pursuers and ran to stand by Rook's Cyclone, one of them crying hysterically.

"'I suppose you degenerates have overrun the whole place since I've been gone,' Rook continued.

"The outlaw riders looked at one another and said nothing. Finally, they laughed and took off, warning Rook that she had made a big mistake in coming back.

"'Skull's right,' I heard one of the women say to Rook. 'You better split. The wars aren't like before. The Red Snakes have five times as many members now.'

"'Five times?...Is Romy doing anything about it? Are the Blue Angels still around?'

"'Broken up,' the other woman said between sobs. 'They've fallen apart. Romy spends all his time with...'

"'Say it, Sue—I already know.'

"'Your sister,' Sue said, lowering her head. 'He can't fight them alone. No one can.' "

"The canyon widened some at its eastern end, where there was a surprisingly well kept park. Rook spent the rest of the night there—what little there was left of it— still unaware that I wasn't fifty feet away from her. In the morning a small van drove into the park; a nonde-script-looking guy and a girl who couldn't have been more than fifteen stepped out, opened up the back, and, for an hour or so, sold and refilled canisters of propane gas for what appeared to be steady customers. Rook watched for some time without revealing herself, until the last customer had been served and the duo was get-ting ready to pack up and leave. Of course it occurred to me that these two might be Romy and Rook's sister, Lilly, but I had no way of being sure until Rook opened her mouth.

"On foot, she had moved her Cyclone to the top of a wide stone staircase that overlooked the couple's busi-ness area and signaled her presence by starting up the mecha. The man looked up at the sound and said, 'Who the heck...?' then, 'Rook!' full of excitement.

"But she returned a cold sneer. 'Romy, how the heck could you just let the Snakes take control of this place?' she demanded.

"'Welcome back,' Romy said, nonplussed.

"'Sue tells me there's five times as many of them as there used to be.'

"'I worried about you, Rook.'

"'Liar!' she shot back. 'I'll bet you were *real* worried about me when Atilla and his Snakes were stomping the hell out of me in a rumble you and the rest of the Angels never attended!'

"'Rook—'

"'How could you have done that to me, Romy?' Rook said, sobbing now. 'If you only knew what they did to me . . . there was no way I could stay here after that.'

"While all this was going on, I saw the girl walk out from behind the van, her hand to her mouth in a startled gesture. Now she spoke to Rook through sobs of her own.

"'You don't understand—it wasn't like that at all!' she began.

Rook's younger sister! I thought. She bore almost no resemblance to her blond sibling. Lilly was raven-haired and petite, dressed in a pleated white skirt and a simple burgundy-colored sweater.

"'Romy didn't run away—he tried to help you, but he was ambushed by the Red Snakes. They beat him up so bad, he couldn't walk for a month. It was the Snakes' plan all along to make it seem like Romy deserted you. They knew you would leave the Angels, and without you, the Angels were nothing. So when you left, everything fell apart.'

"Rook wore a confused look now.

"'That's enough,' Romy was telling Lilly.

"'Please don't blame him,' said Lilly. 'He searched all over for you.'

"Rook looked from one to the other, former lover to sister.

"'Why should I believe you?' she asked. '*Either* of you!'

"Lilly took a step closer. 'Besides, you can't expect Romy to take on the Snakes alone.' She motioned to the delivery van and to Romy, who was tight-lipped and, I think, embarrassed by the scene. 'We're trying to build a life for ourselves, Rook. Romy isn't going to do the stupid things he used to do. He's...he's grown up.'

"I thought Rook was going to take offense at the re-mark, but she didn't. In fact, I could see that she was no longer angry.

"'Sure the Snakes are an evil bunch,' Lilly continued. 'But if you don't give them a *reason* to fight, they mind their own turf. Romy's not holding back because he's a coward, but for the good of *everyone*.'

"Rook smiled. 'So you're holding back, are you, Romy?'

"I'm not sure just what was on Rook's mind—maybe the idea that Romy was also holding back the affection he still had for her. In any case, Lilly answered yes for him, and Rook said that she was beginning to under-stand. 'I guess it took a bookworm to make him see the light,' she directed at Lilly.

"Lilly was about to say something, when one of the girls Rook had rescued appeared at the top of the stair-case. Sue, if I recall.

"'You've got to run for it, Rook!' she said, out of breath. 'The Red Snakes are all over Trenchtown look-ing for you!'

"I saw Rook grin. 'Great!' she said, engaging the Cy-clone. She asked Romy if the Snakes still hung out at something she named 'Highways.' Romy nodded warily. 'Rook, you're not thinking of—'

"'It's what I've been waiting for,' she told him. '*Revenge!*'

"She stomped the Cyclone into gear and raced off, leaving all of us wondering if we would ever see her again."

CHAPTER
ELEVEN

"No one can dispute the accomplishment. The very fact that they undertook the journey [to Reflex Point] is in and of itself a measure of their courage and commitment; the very fact that they journeyed so far through such hostile territory a testament to their skills. But someone needs to point out the troubles the journey stirred up for those along the way. Can anyone name one Southlands settlement that survived their [the Bernard team's] wake?"

Breetai Tul, as quoted in Zeus Bellow, *The Road to Reflex Point*

"**I** DECIDED TO SHOW MYSELF AFTER ROOK SPLIT. I brought the Cyclone to life and pulled out from my place of concealment in the bushes, surprising the hell out of Romy and Lilly. I popped a small wheelie for effect and screeched to a halt, allowing the tail end to slide around to where Romy stood with his mouth half-open.

"'Well, don't just stand there waiting for flies to land,' I said to him. 'Hop on and let's give her some backup support.'

"Romy flashed Lilly a look that communicated several dozen things at once and climbed on. I could tell that Lilly wanted to hold him back, but she knew better than to try. Romy had to get this out of his system for his sake as well as Rook's. I mean, *nobody* likes to be thought of as a Khyron, even if it was all a misunderstanding.

"Cavalierly, I nodded to Lilly and powered the Cyclone up the staircase, getting a rise out of the fact that Romy was white-knuckling the seat grips all the while. I have to admit that I liked impressing would-be motorcycle toughs like Romy; they were an all too frequently encountered breed in the wastes, and I was bored to tears by them.

"Once up top, I asked Romy about this 'Highways' place Rook had mentioned; he shouted directions into my ear, and I wristed the Cyc's throttle, letting it open up along the undamaged sections of roadway that led back to the narrow heart of the city.

"It must have been about this time that the three Invid paid a call on Scott and the others. I had been wondering what they had made of our disappearance from camp. Perhaps they figured we had run off together or just decided that individually we had had enough of Scott's search for Reflex Point. As it came out later, Annie was all for going out to look for us, but Scott felt differently. 'I prefer not to meddle in people's private affairs,' is how Annie told me he had put it. But I guessed correctly that they had opted to hang in for another day, thinking that we would find our way back to them. There was a good chance they would have literally passed right over Trenchtown on their way north, but strangely enough, Scott found his own way to the city in the canyon—with a little help from the Invid, that is.

"They came swooping down on the camp early in the morning, laying waste to that beautiful patch of forest. Whoever was in charge had elected to send in the big guns again: combat ships like the one we had seen after our run-in with the black bear. The team had no chance to hit back, only take cover and keep their heads down. The other thing I learned afterward was that neither the Alpha nor Lancer's Cyclone was activated or otherwise engaged before the attack, which suggested that the combat units had a means of zeroing in on Protoculture even when it wasn't being tapped for energy.

"Scott did manage to make it to the Alpha, though. He brought up the VT's power and launched before the Invid reduced the camp to a fiery ruin, but apparently that was only the first of his woes. The three aliens formed up on his tail and went after him with an unprecedented fury, layering the zone above the forest with unforgiving streams of annihilation discs. When Scott glimpsed Trenchtown's canyon, he saw his out; he led the Invid down into the seemingly deserted city, intent on battling them there.

"Closing on Highways, I heard what I then thought was thunder but later learned were the detonations of the eight heat-seekers Scott had dumped on one of the Invid ships.

"Highways turned out to be the headquarters of the Red Snakes. It was on the roof of a skeletal fifteen-story building, reached by a series of jerry-rigged ramps that connected it with an adjacent (and equally devastated) ten-story parking garage. Romy and I arrived a few moments after Rook, who was braving it out on her own against more than a dozen outlaw bikers. At the center of the group stood the Snakes' main man, a mean-looking hulk named Atilla. He must have stood six six and weighed in at two eighty, most of which was pure muscle. He had a pot, like most of these rogue leaders do, and affected a getup that was part street, part costume, including armless goggles no larger than bottlecaps he had had stitched to his eye sockets, black leather wristbands, shin guards and knee pads fashioned to resemble poised cobras, and a kind of pointed, twin-horned Vikinglike helmet and cowl combination. There was a large S emblazoned on the front of his sleeveless T-shirt, and he had a face not even a mother could love, with a nose that was wide and flattened from countless breaks.

"'I've gotta admit it, Rook,' he was saying as we pulled up. 'You got a lotta guts. It's just too bad you ain't got the brains that go along with it.'

"At that, Atilla gestured to his assembled pack, and they responded with the appropriate litany of hoots and hollers. The implication was clear enough: Rook was about to receive a stomping that would make the first seem like a love fest.

"'I didn't think you had it in you, Rook,' Atilla added.

"But if Rook was at all worried at that moment, she had me fooled. Somewhere along the way she had suited herself up in Cyclone battle armor. But even so, she looked vulnerable, straddling her bike, glaring right back at them, her blond hair mussed by the wind.

"'I'd say *you're* the one who's the coward. Snake Eyes,' she fired back. 'You're nothing without this army of slugs you call a tribe.'

"During this little exchange we were parked on the remains of a roof balcony, above and behind Rook. Romy was eager to go down to her, but I told him to hang back a moment more, at least until the rules were laid down.

"'You're Mr. Mean,' Rook was saying, 'only because you've got the odds on your side, and not one of these rogues has the balls to challenge your position. But I think you're hollow to the core, and I came back here to tell you that.'

"This was the same Rook I had fallen in love with that day in Pops's biker bar . . . And unless Atilla was a lot quicker than the scuz she had seen to there, he was soon to be one sorry rogue, and I knew it.

"To Rook's taunts, Atilla returned something befitting his intellect—something like: 'Oh yeah? Prove it!'—before she got down to the challenge.

"'Just you and me,' she told him. 'One on one, right here in front of all your boys. And I'll even make it easy for you. We won't even fight; we'll just have a chicken race.'

"'A race?' Atilla roared laughingly. 'I thought we were gonna have some fun.'

"Rook grinned and said, 'The beam,' pointing to something off to her left.

"This brought a real chorus of cheers from the spectators. I didn't understand what she was talking about until Romy showed me what the beam was. It was either the remains of a bridge that had once linked Highways with the building across the street or a collapsed structural member from one of the two buildings. In any case, it was no more than foot wide and now ran roof to roof more than one hundred and fifty feet above the city's main street. But that wasn't all: The beam was not entirely straight. Midway along was a bend and a slight dip—from who knew what—to test the mettle of any rider. Reaching the beam first was only part of the game; reaching the other roof was something else again. It was obvious from everyone's reactions that the beam was one of Trenchtown's rites of passage, an initiation that had certainly ended in more than one death.

"While I was taking all of this in, Romy was dismounting from the Cyclone. 'We can't let her go through with this,' he told me, showing an intense anger that almost led me to reevaluate my initial impression of him.

"Atilla, meanwhile, was doing his best to back away from the challenge without losing face. He pointed out to his assembled buddies that what he had envisioned was a genuine physical mix-up with Rook—winner taking all, so to speak—and they were buying it.

"'Let's pluck this chicken *now*!' he shouted, leering at Rook.

"I could understand his misgivings, but if I were him I would have been pointing out the fact that Rook's Cyclone was not only faster than his old Kamikaze but capable of reconfiguring and actually *flying* across to the opposite roof should Rook misjudge the beam itself. Well, perhaps he had never seen a Cyclone before, I thought.

"Romy and I were standing side by side on the roof balcony now. Below, Atilla and his Huns were beginning to take a fancy to the idea of jumping Rook's bones, so I decided it was time for us to show our colors, pulled out the hand H–90, and fired off a quick vertical burst for the boys that stopped them dead in their tracks.

"'Stay where you are!' I warned them, feeling a little like Atilla with the blaster backing up my threats. 'The two of them fight it out alone, just like the lady says.' Rook was more surprised by my sudden appearance than any of them. I figured that by backing her I was doing a little better than Romy, who was now urging her to give up the idea. His presence elicited as many comments from the Snakes as Rook's idea of riding the beam had. It seemed that the former leader of the Blue Angels was not very well thought of in the Snakes' side of town.

"'Don't worry, Romy, I won't blow it,' Rook was saying, not entirely successful at hiding her concern. 'Let's just say my riding skills have improved a lot.' She looked hard at Romy and thanked him for standing by her. 'Coming back here was a good thing,' she said, smiling. 'I think it cleared my head of a lot of bad memories. More than you'll ever know. . .'

"'Rook,' Romy started to say.

"'I'm counting on you to take care of Lilly,' Rook added, activating the Cyc.

"I walked down the stairs and casually aimed the blaster in Atilla's direction. 'You gonna run this race, or what?' I asked him, unsure about my next move should he refuse.

"The Snakes threw words of encouragement to their leader, and Atilla stepped forward to accept the challenge. Romy ceremoniously handed Rook her helmet, and some of the Snakes ran to the edge of the roof for a better view of the race.

"Things got under way without the preliminaries and fanfare that usually characterize such events; Rook and Atilla positioned their machines on either side of a flag bearer, maybe a hundred feet from the beam. The starter, a shaved-skull Snake in T-shirt and fatigues, jumped up and brought the flag down with a shout. The two machines patched out and headed for the beam. Again, I thought I heard distant thunder but made nothing of it.

"I had noticed Atilla give the red Cyc a dismissive once-over before the flag dropped and figured he would be in for a surprise. But I was the one surprised: The old Kami was a real sleeper and must have concealed a turbocharger somewhere within its works, because Atilla beat Rook off the line and stayed a half length ahead of her for the first fifty feet. In fact, I'm pretty sure Snake Eyes would have hit the beam neck and neck with Rook if fear hadn't revealed his own true colors.

"Just shy of the beam he glanced over at Rook, saw that she wasn't about to yield an inch, and bailed out, bouncing and sliding all the way, his cycle plummeting over the edge and exploding when it hit the street.

"Rook rode the beam like a pro. She told me later that at no time did she even consider using the mecha's capabilities to save herself from wiping out. I ran forward to the edge of the roof, along with everyone else who was applauding her feat, including more than a few Snakes. The loyal members of the gang were ministering to their bruised and road-rashed leader, who knew, I think, that many more challenges would soon be coming his way.

"Rook had raised the faceshield of the helmet and was waving back to us when I realized that that distant thunder was no longer either distant or thunder. And an instant later, we saw Scott streak overhead in the Alpha, pursued by two Invid combat ships. The Snakes began to freak and scatter for cover. I turned and heard one of them shout: 'They found out about the Protoculture I stole! They're gonna blow us apart!'

"I looked back at Rook in time to see her spin the Cyc through a 360, accelerate along the roof, and launch herself into Battle Armor mode. This was lost on most of the Snakes, but I noticed Atilla staring at the transformed Cyclone like he had just witnessed some kind of miracle.

"Rook put down on a roof a few blocks down the canyon, raised the mecha's cannon, and took out one of the ships. Scott, at the same time, had thrown the VT into a booster climb and was now falling back down upon the second, unleashing a rain of six missiles to deal with the thing. The Invid dropped itself to street level, dodging as best it could, but ultimately took one of the heat-seekers full force and spun out of control, impaling itself on a spiked piece of construction infrastructure. You would have thought Rook and Scott had planned it that way."

"After the action died down, I used the Cyc's tac net to notify Scott that his errant troops would be home soon; we made plans to rendezvous on the north road.

"I didn't have any doubts about Rook's bidding a swift good-bye to Trenchtown, even though some wrongs had now been redressed and some old worries laid to rest. But I knew also that there was still a scene that had to be played out with Romy, and I was anxious to see it.

"The four of us—me, Rook, Romy, and Lilly—got together for eats at his place. Small talk for the most part; Romy made no mention of Rook's staying on in

Trenchtown, and we made no mention of Reflex Point, Lancer, or the others.

"'Rook, it's been so good seeing you again,' Lilly said as we were preparing to shove off. 'I just can't tell you ... If it hadn't been for your courage, the Snakes would still be ruling this city...' She started getting weepy about then, and it made Rook angry.

"'What on Earth are you crying about?' Rook said, putting her hands on the smaller woman's shoulders. When Lilly exchanged looks with Romy, Rook caught on and lightened up. 'Hey, don't worry about me,' she told Lilly. 'There's a person in my life now who means a lot to me...'

"I was leaning against the building with my hands behind my head when she suddenly turned to me. 'Rand,' she said, leadingly and with a sweetness that didn't fit her. She came over and took hold of my arm, finding a pressure point in my wrist at the same time. 'Come on, give me a kiss like you always do.' Under her breath, she told me to pretend to be her honey or else. 'Kiss me on the cheek—and make it look good,' she added.

"Romy and Lilly were watching with a mixture of bemusement and anticipation, and Rook was standing there, offering me her left cheek like she was my aunt or something, so I did what I had to do to make it look good! I took hold of her upper arms and pulled her to me before she even had a chance to close her mouth. I didn't hold her long, and she kept her eyes wide for the duration, not returning the favor, but it was long enough to bring a scarlet blush to her cheeks.

"'Rook is my baby and always will be,' I told Romy over Rook's shoulder, putting some bass in my voice to keep from laughing. 'Come on, honey. Let's get back to the ranch,' I said as I mounted my Cyc.

"Rook climbed on her mecha without looking at me. Lilly started to say something, but Rook just said good-bye and motored off. I did the same, leaving Romy and Lilly in the street, his arm draped over her narrow shoulders.

"When I came alongside Rook, she flashed me the anger she didn't want to show in front of her sister, and I decided to have some fun with it. 'You kiss pretty well for such a tough gal,' I ribbed her.

"'That was supposed to be the *cheek*, dirtbag.'

"'Jeez, I'm sorry...I must have misunderstood or something...'

"'Pea brain! Degenerate!'

"I laughed, then tried to switch tracks. 'What about your folks, Rook?' I asked her. 'Are they still living in this hole?' I was sincere about it; Rook's past was my way into her present.

"But she just shook her head and made for the conduit, not bothering to look behind."

CHAPTER
TWELVE

*The book Lunk had promised to deliver was called In-
herit the Stars, a piece of speculative fiction written by the
noted twentieth-century British author and inventor James P.
Hogan and first published in 1977. It was the first in a series
of novels that dealt with humankind's contact with an alien
race indigenous to Ganymede (the Ganymeans), who in
many ways were the antithesis of the Opteran Invid.*

Footnote in Xandu Reem, *A Stranger at Home: A
Biography of Scott Bernard*

WHEN THEY WERE REUNITED AND ON THE ROAD
north once again, it was business as usual. Four hundred
miles north of Trenchtown the team was attacked by five
Invid Troopers, which they disposed of almost without
breaking stride. Scott took out the first two from the
Alpha and left the rest of the work to the three Cyclones,
piloted by Rook, Rand, and Lancer, who had by now
become a finely honed unit. There had been no signs of
Pincer ships for several days, and though the Troopers
were bothersome, they posed no real threat provided
that each one glimpsed was accounted for on the battle-
field.

The desert terrain helped them to easily spot the
Troopers. They had left the highlands behind. Gone were
the forests and misshapen buttes of those plateaus, as
well as the cool air and sparkling rivers they had come to

take for granted. But this was not true desert, waterless and unforgiving, but rather a broad expanse of arid lowland, with solitary flat-topped mesas to break the monotony of the horizon and enough spring-fed lakes to support a wide assortment of settlements.

Lunk, demanding equal-time benefits after Rook's "dalliance in the Trench"—Rand's words—was calling the shots on the latest detour along the way. The group was headed toward a town called Roca Negra, sixty miles west of the north road and said to be a community that had managed to retain an old-world charm.

The team had an overview of the place now from the tableland a few miles east. Roca Negra looked neat and compact, enlivened by groupings of cottonwood and eucalyptus trees, and lent a certain drama by the mesa and rounded peaks that all but overshadowed it. Scott made a pass over the town in the Alpha, the VT's deltalike shadow paralleling the course of the main road, and reported his sightings. There was a large circular fountain and plaza central to the town, with an assortment of rustic-style buildings grouped around it and the few streets that radiated out from the hub like the spokes of a wheel. Scott could make out tile roofs and cobblestone streets, a church steeple, and a number of people, some of whom were staring up at the Veritech, while others ran off to inform the rest of the townsfolk.

Lunk smiled at the thought of the place and urged the van along with added throttle. Annie was next to him in the shotgun seat. It was the same police van they had commandeered in Norristown, but Lunk had removed the canvas top and given the thing an olive-drab once-over in memory of the beloved APC he had had blown out from under him in the highlands. Lancer, Rook, and Rand flanked the truck on their Cyclones.

"I sure hope we'll be able to get some food in this town," Annie said after Scott's message. "I'm starved!"

Lunk flashed her a bright-eyed smile and told her not to worry, then turned to Rand, who had come alongside on the driver's side of the van.

"What's so special 'bout this place?" Rand shouted into the wind. "You been here before?"

Lunk shook his head, maintaining the smile.

"Then why are we stopping here?" Annie demanded, joining in.

Lunk reached back and pulled a worn paperback book from the rear pocket of his fatigues, holding it out the window for Rand's inspection.

"To make good a promise I made to a friend a year ago," Lunk said to both of them. "To deliver this book."

Rand gazed at the thing but couldn't make out much, except that it was aged, yellowed, dog-eared, and smudged. Someone had thought to wrap the book in protective plastic, but too late to preserve the cover illustration.

"What sort of book is it?" Rand asked.

Lunk pulled the book in and regarded it. "I really don't know—I haven't read it. But it was important enough to my buddy for him to ask me to bring it to his father if I ever got the chance."

"Well, why didn't your buddy deliver it himself, if it's so important?"

"I wish he could. . . ."

Rand saw Lunk's smile fade and asked him about it.

"It was during the Invid invasion," Lunk began. "My friend was on recon patrol, and I was detailed to rendezvous with him for the extraction. When I found him, he was trying to get away from a couple of Shock Troopers, and I could see he was wounded. They blasted him again while I . . . sat and watched. How he could get up and run after that I'll never know, but he did, and started for the APC. I thought there might still be a chance, but the Invid caught up with him before I could move in, and he didn't have a prayer."

Annie could see that Lunk was torturing himself with the memory ~~but~~ kept still and allowed him to finish. Was this what he had run from? Annie wondered, recalling comments uttered months ago when they had first met.

"He called out to me," Lunk was saying. "Calling me to come get him, but there was *nothing I could do*. The Invid had spotted the APC and started after me, and I had no choice but to make a run for it.

"I don't even remember how I got away from them . . . But I can still hear my buddy's voice coming over the net, as loud and clear today as I heard it then, calling me to help him. I can't forget . . ."

Lunk's face was beaded with sweat, and Annie fought down an urge to hold him. But he was through it now and sort of shaking himself back to the present, looking hard at the book again.

"This had some special meaning for him, I suppose. The one thing he wanted most was for his old man to have it. I promised on the day he went out . . ."

"Oh, Lunk," Annie broke in, touching his arm lightly. "You've been carrying more than that book around, haven't you? I feel so bad. . . ."

Rand looked in through the driver's side and noticed Annie crying. "Lunk," he said all of a sudden. "We've got a book to deliver. So let's get on it!"

Lunk saw Rand wrist the Cyclone's throttle to wheelie the mecha into lead position. He smiled to himself, thankful for the company of his friends, and pressed his foot down on the van's accelerator pedal.

* * *

Roca Negra had a secret of its own, a dirty little secret compared to the one Lunk wore like a scarlet letter. But no one on the team was aware of this just yet; the only thing immediately obvious was that the town seemed deserted despite Scott's recent claims to the contrary.

"Where is everybody?" Lancer said to Rook and Rand as the three Cyclones entered the empty plaza.

"What'd you expect—the welcome wagon?" Rook asked sarcastically. "After all, we didn't tell them Yellow Dancer was coming to town. It's probably just siesta time."

Rand took a look around the circle, certain he saw people ducking away from the open windows and pulling shutters closed on others. Even the central fountain was deserted, but the damp earth around it suggested that people had been there a short time ago. "You don't find this a bit *strange*?" he asked Rook.

"You're both imagining things," she said. "It's not like this hasn't happened before. Besides, there are two kids right over there," she added, pointing to two young boys munching on apples nearby.

Rand relaxed somewhat at that and swung his mecha into a second lap around the well. He began to take stock of the buildings now and realized that his expectations had been way off base: Instead of the stucco and terra-cotta village he had envisioned, Roca Negra was like something lifted from what used to be called England. The architecture was of a style he had heard referred to as Tudor, with mullioned windows, tall gables, nogging and timber facades, and steeply pitched tiled roofs. "How about giving me a bite?" he heard Annie shout to the kids as the van drove past them. Then he spotted the restaurant: José's Café, according to the sign above the curved entryway.

Rook, Lancer, and Lunk followed Rand's lead, but only Lunk moved in to investigate. There were tables and chairs set up out front but no one on the scene to serve them.

"Bring me some peppermint candies!" Annie shouted to Lunk.

Lunk turned briefly to acknowledge her, and when he swung around, there was a mustachioed man standing in the restaurant's barroom swinging doors.

"The restaurant is closed during the emergency," the man began. He spoke with a Spanish accent and wore an apron and work shirt more suited to the trades than to the food biz, but he was gesturing Lunk to halt in a way that suggested he owned the place. "Our communications have been cut, and we're short on supplies of all kinds. The indications right now are that we'll be closed for about a month."

"But we've traveled such a long way!" Annie shouted out the open top of the van, disappointment in her voice. "We haven't had a decent meal in weeks."

"I told you what the situation is," the man fired back, raising his fist. Lunk was taken aback by the gesture. The man was slight, but his dark eyes were flashing with an anger that seemed to add to his aspect. "There's nothing I can do about it. We have no food to feed you. I suggest that you try the next town."

The man had moved past Lunk and was now overturning the café chairs and placing them legs up on the table. Lunk followed him, deciding to steer clear of the food issue for a moment and inquire as to the whereabouts of Alfred Nader, his dead friend's father. But the simple question seemed to unhinge the restaurant owner, who dropped one of the chairs at the mention of the man's name.

"What're you getting so upset about?" Lunk asked, concerned but not yet suspicious. "I only want to know how I can find Alfred Nader's house. Is that too much to ask, or are you as short on information as you are on food?"

The owner averted Lunk's penetrating gaze and busied himself righting the chair. "You must have the wrong town," he said distractedly. "I know everyone in town, and there's nobody named Nader living here."

"But you must have heard of him," Lunk pressed. "Alfred Nader? . . ."

"I tell you I never heard of him," the man said, raising his voice and moving back toward the swinging doors. "Now go away and leave me alone!"

"This is weird," Lunk said, turning around to face Rand and the others. "This guy tells me Alfred Nader doesn't live here. But he's lying, I'm sure of it." Lunk took a look back at the doorway and walked to the van. "Why the heck would he lie like that?"

"Something stinks," said Lancer. "Nader's here. We're just going to have to find him on our own."

"We'll split up," Rook suggested.

"All right, I'll go with Lunk," said Rand, already climbing into the van's shotgun seat. "We'll meet in an hour by the bridge outside town."

Lunk thanked his friends for their support and got behind the wheel. He swung the van around and headed it out of the plaza, followed closely by Rook and Lancer, who both ignored Annie's attempts to team up with them.

"Well, screw you guys!" she yelled as they roared off; then she spied Rand's untended Cyclone and smiled broadly.

* * *

Lunk and Rand headed up one of the streets leading from the plaza. There were a few people about, but without exception they disappeared as the van approached. Shutters slammed overhead, women carried their children indoors, and men shouted threats from the darkness of interior spaces. Much to Rand's surprise, Lunk seemed to know his way.

"My friend used to tell me all about this place," Lunk explained, a bit nostalgic. "He'd tell me all about his father, about how his old man was a big shot in town—a politician or something."

"And the restaurant owner never heard of him, huh?" Rand said knowingly. "What are they trying to cover up?"

"There's supposed to be a bakery somewhere along this street," Lunk said, leaving Rand's question unanswered and looking around. "There it is," he said a moment later. "A few more landmarks and I might be able to find my way to Nader's house without anybody's help."

Rand was silent while Lunk took one turn after another, the pattern of disappearances and threats unbroken. "You know, something just occurred to me," he said to Lunk when they had reached the outskirts of town. "Maybe they're trying to protect Nader."

"How do you mean?" Lunk asked, pulling the van over.

Rand turned to him. "These people don't know us. For all they know we could be sympathizers. If Nader was a politico, he could be in trouble."

"With who?"

Rand shrugged. "The Invid, for starters."

The rest of the team, having met with the same reception, had abandoned their search and were killing time at the edge of town, waiting for Lunk and Rand to show up.

Rook was on her feet, leaning almost casually against the stone wall of the bridge. Lancer and Annie were sitting on the grassy embankment above the stream.

"Lunk and Rand have got to pass by here eventually," Lancer was telling the others.

Rook agreed. "We're better off just waiting for them. But one of us is going to have to find Scott. Where do you think he put the Alpha down? . . . Hey! A truck!" she said suddenly. "Maybe the driver can shed some light on this thing."

Annie turned to glance at the truck. "Looks like they're stopping."

No one moved as the truck came to a halt on the bridge. They had seen two men in the cab and were looking there, when without warning a third man jumped from the canvased rear. It took them a moment to realize that he was wearing a gas mask and what looked like a twin-tanked oxyacetylene rig on his back. And by the time they had made sense of this it was too late: The man had brought the rig's torch out front and released a foul-smelling, eye-smarting gas into their midst.

Almost immediately Rook and Lancer began to cough uncontrollably. Beneath the cloud and consequently somewhat less affected by it, Annie tried to slide down the embankment and reach the stream. But the gas's effects caught up with her; she felt a searing pain work its way toward her lungs and doubled up into a fit of coughing. The cloud was as dense as smoke, but she could discern that several other men had followed the lead man from the back of the truck. They, too, had gas masks on, but they also carried bats and clubs. Just before Annie went under, she saw Rook and Lancer fall as roundhouse blows were directed against them.

* * *

There was an olive tree and a small circular well where there should have been a house. Otherwise the lot was empty, the buildings that surrounded it on three sides burned and abandoned. Puzzled, Lunk stood staring at the scene.

"Are you sure this is the place?" Rand asked him from the van. He had pulled out one of the former police vehicle's air-cooled autopistols and was resting it up against his collarbone now.

"Yep. He told me his dad had a well and an olive tree in his backyard. And there they are. Now all we have to do is find the house."

Rand frowned and stepped away from the van to join his friend. "There's got to be twenty houses in this town with an olive tree and a well in the backyard, Lunk. And even if this was Nader's place, he's obviously not here now. I don't know," Rand added skeptically. "Maybe he's dead, and that's why everybody's acting so strange."

Lunk was starting to reply when Rand heard the sound of footsteps behind him. He looked over his shoulder and found himself facing half a dozen angry-looking men, one of whom was carrying a kind of back-packed welding torch.

Rand swung back around, putting all he had into knocking Lunk to one side while he threw himself in the opposite direction. Lunk took the full force of the gas cloud in the back, but before the men could move in, Rand was through his roll and taking aim at the torch. He pulled off one quick shot that effectively decapitated the twin-spouted rod and gave the men pause. They began to scatter as Rand squeezed off three more shots, one toward the feet of each of the men who were standing guard by the van. The three leapt through a kind of impromptu dance and fled along with their comrades.

Rand called to Lunk and made a beeline for the van, throwing himself into the shotgun seat through the passenger-side door, Lunk just steps behind him.

Off to one side, the men were rallying for another attack.

"Make tracks!" Rand yelled, pounding a fist against the dash.

"You make good sense, buddy!" Lunk yelled back, putting the pedal to the metal.

CHAPTER
THIRTEEN

It has yet to be demonstrated that the Invid Regis was capable of direct dealings with each of her remote drones— Scouts, Troopers and Pincer Ships—prior to Scott Bernard's forcing her hand, so to speak. Commentators have pointed to the incident at Roca Negra as an example of changes in the previous hierarchical organization, in which each hive queen (sic) was made responsible for her own soldiers.

Bloom Nesterfig, *Social Organization of the Invid*

IN JOSÉ'S CAFÉ THE CHURLISH MAYOR OF ROCA Negra, a large, mustachioed man named Pedro, received word of the brutal attack on Rook, Annie, and Lancer.

"They beat them up!" he bellowed now, bringing his big fist down on one of the tables and rising to his full height of six foot four. His English, like José's, had a Spanish accent.

"Yes," José's wife, Maria, continued. She was a small, pretty woman who usually wore her auburn hair in a loose braid over one shoulder. "They put the three of them in the back of the truck, and then they sped off somewhere. But I think the two others got away."

José watched his wife from across the room but said nothing. It worried him to have her interfere in these matters, but she had been adamant about reporting the attack to the mayor, and when she was decided about something, there was nothing José could do to stop her. He only hoped that the rogues who captured the three strangers would not learn of her statements.

"Those no-good bums have done it this time," said Pedro, starting for the door.

Maria's thin hands were clutched at her breast. "You won't let them hurt the others, then?"

"When I get my hands on them, I'll *show* them who runs this town!" the mayor said without looking back.

José watched the doors swing to and fro. *Who* would he show? he asked himself. The rogues or the strangers who had come in search of Alfred Nader? Roca Negra could so easily fall victim to violence from either side....

Meanwhile, Rand and Lunk were speeding toward the bridge to rendezvous with Lancer and the others, unaware that the bad part of town had already come calling.

"But why would they attack us?" Rand asked. "Just to drive us out of town, or what? And where the heck is Scott, anyway?"

"It has something to do with the disappearance of old man Nader," Lunk said firmly. He had the book out again and was regarding it while he drove.

"If that's true, we oughta rethink your idea of trying to get that book to him," Rand suggested.

Lunk shook his big head. "Uh uh, buddy, no way. I said I'd deliver this thing no matter what the odds. And if Nader's alive, I'll find 'im."

"Bravo," Rand replied, crossing his arms. "I just hope you don't get us both killed in the process." The van was closing in on the bridge now, and Lancer was nowhere to be seen. "They're supposed to be here. Where are they?"

"No sign of the Cyclones either," Lunk added, bringing the van to a halt and climbing out. He looked over toward the embankment, then down at tire marks in the dirt road—marks that didn't belong to the van. "Check this out," he told Rand. "Something's been by here earlier on—a truck by the looks of it."

Rand and Lunk bent down to inspect the tracks and in so doing took no notice of the men who climbed up from under the bridge. But Rand had thought to bring the autopistol with him and raised it threateningly as the men advanced. However, a second group joined the first after a moment, and although underarmed with clubs, axes, and farm tools, they stood fourteen strong.

"Some of you are gonna go down with me," Rand warned.

He was standing back to back with Lunk at the center of the wide circle that was forming around them.

"Get a load of this big bruiser with the knife," Rand heard Lunk say. He had no intention of turning around for a look but had to wonder about the size of the man if Lunk was calling him big. "If ever there was an *hombre* with no sense of humor, he's it."

"Well, this character with the ax isn't exactly my idea of a comedian either," Rand answered to let Lunk know how things were on his side of the circle.

"Ugly bunch of gorillas . . ." Lunk growled, lowering himself into a crouch and beckoning one of the men to come in on him.

"What are they waiting for?" Rand started to say, when one of the circle said, "We have your friends."

Rand felt Lunk straighten up behind him. "Throw the weapon down," Lunk told him.

"We're just going to let them take us?"

Lunk already had his massive arms raised. "Take it easy," he said to Rand under his breath. "My guess is they'll take us to Lancer and the girls. Then we'll make our getaway, all right with you?"

. "Well, if you say so . . ." Rand gulped and tossed the autopistol to the dirt, much to the amazement of the circle. "It's your party," he shrugged as the men moved in to bind his wrists.

A short while later, in the back of the same truck that had surprised Lancer, Rook, and Annie at the bridge, Lunk had a change of heart. The truck had entered the plaza and was moving slowly past José's Café. Lunk spotted the owner standing in the doorway and said: "There's that bird José! I bet he knows where our friends are!"

And the next thing Rand knew, Lunk was standing up and shouldering his way toward the street. Rand jumped out of the truck and was right behind him. As the two of them rolled, got to their feet, and made a mad dash for the café entrance, propelled by blasts from the very weapon Rand had surrendered only moments before.

Lunk crashed through the swinging doors at full speed, knocking frail-looking José halfway across the room.

"I sometimes have my doubts about you, partner!" Rand said, out of breath and dodging blasts that were entering the bar from the street. The truck was backing up, disgorging men who were already closing in on the café. "Hope you have another plan ready," he added, noticing for the first time that there was a woman in the room.

Lunk was behind the bar, cutting the cords that bound his hands with a knife he had gripped between his teeth. José was cross-legged on the floor, shaking his head as if to restore himself to consciousness. The woman was kneeling beside him. Lunk freed himself and tossed the knife to Rand, who had to catch it in both hands and duplicate his friend's Houdini act.

"Okay, what's next?" Rand managed with his mouth full.

Lunk grinned and pulled a hand blaster from beneath his shirt. "Surprise," he said, shoving the weapon into José's ribs. "Now, my closed-mouthed friend, you're going to do a little talking."

Rand took a cautious look out the swinging doors and turned to Lunk. "I hate to bring up an unpleasant subject, but there's quite a crowd gathering out there, and since we've only got one blast—"

"In a minute," Lunk cut him off. "Start talking," he said to José, ignoring the pleas of the man's wife.

José swallowed hard. "What about? It isn't my problem."

"You can begin with where our friends are—and no stalling!"

"Maria," he said, looking imploringly at his wife. "What should I do?"

"Please believe us," she told Lunk from her husband's side. "We don't know what became of your friends. Only Pedro knows what happened to them."

"Fine. So produce Pedro."

"He is the mayor," Maria continued. "He's giving all the orders."

"Maria!" José yelled, trying to stop her.

"Then take us to him—*now*!"

"But how?" said José. "We can't get past that mob." He gestured toward the door.

"I've got an idea," Rand said from the door. "José, you've put on a pretty good act so far, and now you're going to do some acting on our behalf. . . ."

José pulled Rand and Lunk through the café's swinging doors a few minutes later, leading them along on a leather leash. Their hands were now bound in front of them with white cloth napkins Maria had helped to knot, one of which dutifully concealed Lunk's blaster. The townsmen were suitably impressed (if somewhat bewildered) and moved in to retake custody of their prisoners, but José waved them off.

"Pedro has asked me to take them to him. He wants you men to stay here and capture their companion when he shows up."

"You're doing fine," Lunk complimented him under his breath. "Now just keep walking. Get us out of here and you'll save your skin. Tell the driver to take us to Pedro."

José motioned to the idling van one of the villagers had driven in from the bridge. "Is this their vehicle?"

The man behind the wheel nodded. José shoved his prisoners into the rear seats and joined them there. Maria rode shotgun.

"Be alert for their comrade," José reminded the men as he ordered the van off.

Away from the café, Lunk loosed the cloth knot and brought the blaster out for the driver to see. He ordered José and the driver out of the van when they reached the mayor's offices.

"Now don't get any funny ideas when we get inside," Lunk advised them, making his point with the weapon. "I don't want to hurt anybody, but I'll do what's necessary."

"You want me, too?" said the driver, Gomez.

"You, too," said Rand, giving him a light shove.

The building was a wooden two-story structure with tall, curved-top entry doors. Lunk and Rand stayed behind the two men as they climbed the staircase to the upper floor, but once at the office, José and Gomez burst through the doors shouting warnings to their friends inside. Lunk was only a step behind them, though, and fired a shot at the ceiling to quiet the room.

There were a dozen or so townspeople in the office,

not counting Lancer, Rook, and Annie, who were bound hand and foot on the floor in the center of the spacious room.

"Hands up!" Lunk bellowed.

"Well, hello, boys," said Rook as plaster rained down on her from Lunk's ceiling shot.

"Where's Scott?" Lancer asked.

Rand moved in to free his friends while Lunk threatened to air-condition the room unless someone directed him to the mayor.

"That's me," said a large man seated at a table.

"Be careful, Pedro," José warned him.

Lunk leveled the blaster at him. "We've got a few questions for you."

"Like where you hid the Cyclones," Rand said, moving to Lunk's side. Lancer and Rook had some nasty bruises, and a new anger was evident in Rand's voice.

But the mayor wasn't impressed. "We have them, and we mean to keep them," he told Rand. "You people are free to go, but we keep the machines."

Rand showed his teeth. "Hear me, mister, and hear me good: We're giving the orders now, not you."

"Give all the orders you want, but we'll do what we have to do."

Rand made an impatient sound and grabbed the blaster from Lunk's hands. "Talk to him, Lunk, before I do something I might regret."

The big man nodded and stepped forward. "All right, Mr. Mayor, forget the Cyclones for a moment. What I want now is the truth about Alfred Nader."

"I don't know anyone named Nader," Pedro said, meeting Lunk's glare. But the stifled gasps from others in the room told a different story.

Lunk slammed his fists down on the table. "I'm sick of listening to lies, pal!"

Rand put a hand on his friend's arm. "Hold on a minute," he started to say. But suddenly the building was shaking. Annie pointed at the window: Rand saw flashes of brilliant orange light in the skies above the mesa.

"Annihilation discs!" said Rand. "Invid patrol ships!"

"Now at least we know where Scott's been," Lancer chimed in.

Rand turned to the mayor, furious now.

"Your time is up, Pedro! We need those Cyclones!"

The mayor remained tight-lipped. "We don't want any more fighting in our village."

"If we don't get out there and help our friend, there won't *be* any more village," Lancer pointed out.

Pedro scoffed at him. "Do you imagine you heroes are going to repel an Invid attack by yourselves?"

"You better let us try," Rand said as the sounds of distant explosions infiltrated the room.

"I mustn't endanger the town!"

"We're trying to *help* your town," Rook told him.

Lunk took the blaster back from Rand and raised it. "That tears it! I'm not standing by while my friend dies for this stinking excuse for a town. Pedro, you've got ten seconds!"

"Wait!" José said, stepping into the projected line of fire. He turned to Gomez. "Tell them where the Cyclones are hidden."

"You're responsible for this, José," the mayor shouted. "If anything should happen to our village—"

"I'll take the responsibility then," José answered, whirling on him.

"They're in the warehouse," Gomez said softly.

The warehouse was a barn situated close to the bridge, an odds-and-ends storage facility for grain, farming tools, and rusting examples of early Robotechnology. The Cyclones had been rolled into a corner and covered over with a couple of mildewed canvas tarps.

Lancer, Rook, and Rand headed straight for their machines, activated them, and rode off to the sound of the guns. Annie and Lunk wished them luck and watched as the Cyclones reconfigured to Battle Armor mode. Lunk was heading back to the van when he heard his name called. It was Pedro, looking somewhat sheepish and conciliatory.

"Lunk, you're determined to go through with this?"

Lunk gestured to the by-now-distant Cyclones and said harshly, "That oughta answer your question."

Pedro nodded sullenly. "Then there's something I want you to see," he said, leading Lunk back into the barn. Inside, he motioned to an object concealed under a nylon cloth and pulled the cover away.

"I want you to have this."

Lunk knew it by its slang term—a "Stinger"—a lightweight autocannon no larger than a turn-of-the-century M-70 machine gun that ran on Protoculture and delivered piercing bursts of Reflex firepower. Stingers were the weapon of choice for the resistance early on, but with the Invid's control of Protoculture, the weapon had passed quickly into disuse. This one looked as though it had never been fired, but it hadn't been well cared for either.

"This was given to our town by a group of freedom fighters," Pedro began to explain while Lunk inspected the gun. "Before I was mayor, when...Nader was alive." Lunk straightened up at the mention of the name.

Pedro's voice took on a harder edge. "But Nader didn't want it used. He actually believed we could make a separate peace with the Invid and hid the gun, afraid that fighting back would end in death for all of us. But many of the townspeople misinterpreted his concern; they accused him of cowardice and worse. When he still wouldn't reveal where he had hidden the thing...they beat him to death. They burned his home, they..."

Lunk saw that Pedro was sobbing. "So that's your dirty little secret . . . the reason why those men attacked us. You're all ashamed of what happened here."

Pedro nodded. "May God have mercy on us. By the time we found the gun, it was too late to do anything. The Invid had overrun everything."

"And now you're the one who feels responsible for this place. You've inherited Nader's legacy."

"You could say that."

Lunk's hard look softened. "Pedro, maybe I've misjudged you."

"And I, you," returned the mayor. "A common enough mistake these days."

Out on the flats things were looking grim for Scott and the team. The arrival of the Cyclones had taken the pressure off him to some extent, but the Invid still outnumbered them three to one.

Shock Troopers again. Scott wasn't sure why they had showed up. It was possible that one of the Scouts they had tangled with earlier had gotten away. He had seen the first of the Troopers just as the team had been entering Roca Negra and had doubled back to deal with it. But on the tail of the first came a second, then a third and a fourth, and before Scott knew it, he was in the midst of a full contingent of Pincer units.

He dropped the Alpha in for a release run now, going after three grounded Invid who had pinned down Rook and Rand with cannon fire. The already cratered and fused terrain was being torn up by annihilation discs, the air above superheated and crosshatched by missile tracks launched from the Cyclones' forearm tubes. Scott loosed a flock of heat-seekers at the bottom of his dive and climbed sharply, looking back over his right shoulder to catch a glimpse of the results of his run. Two

Invid ships were flaming wrecks, collapsed and bleeding green nutrient. Another was badly damaged but still on its feet, one of its pincers blown away.

Scott swung his head as he thought the Alpha through a roll and saw Lunk's van streaking across the sands, seemingly on a collision course with three more Invid ships. Alert to the van's approach, the Troopers lifted off, forming up in a triangular pattern to deal with it.

But in a moment it was obvious that they had misjudged Lunk.

Scott caught sight of a brilliant flash at the front of the van an instant before one of the ships exploded in midair. A second flash and another Invid was blown to pieces. Scott realized that Lunk had mounted some sort of cannon to the van. Apparently the Invid also recognized the weapon, because they were suddenly giving the van a wide berth. Rook, Rand, and Lancer took advantage of the opportunity to deal out death blows of their own, managing to fell two additional Troopers with precision shots to the ships' optic scanners.

Scott smiled broadly and uttered a short, triumphant cry to the skies outside the Alpha's canopy. Not only had they cut the odds, they had won the battle.

The remaining Invid were actually turning tail and fleeing the area!

It was the first time Scott had ever seen them retreat.

Lunk returned to Roca Negra alone. He had a longer talk with Pedro and José about Alfred Nader. Both men had known Nader's son, Lunk's friend, and were sorry to hear that he had been killed.

The battle on the flats hadn't affected the rest of the town's attitude toward Lunk, but he understood this and pitied them the cross they had to bear. He had his own, and the emotional weight of it hadn't been lessened any by this brief stop at Roca Negra. In fact, he felt even more confused than before. Would Nader have turned out to be a sympathizer in the end? Would his town have been just another place where the people were too busy maintaining their separate peace to rally to the cause of a greater one?

Lunk spent some private time at what had once been Nader's ranch, picking up ripened olives from the tree and drinking cool water from the well. Lunk kept the book. More than the object of a promise now, it had become a symbol of confusion, of mistrust and treachery . . . markings engraved upon Earth's tortured and embattled landscape and upon the very fabric of Human life.

FOURTEEN

Psychohistorian Adler Ripple traces Jonathan Wolff's treachery to his illicit affair with Lynn-Minmei. He had met her on Little Luna (the Robotech factory satellite), during the Hunters' wedding and fallen in love with her while the two of them were, for all intents and purposes, stranded on Tirol. It's likely they would have married had the Sentinels not come between them. (Minmei had vowed to steer clear of soldiers after her brief and disastrous fling with Rick Hunter. Ironically, she caught the bridal bouquet at Hunter's wedding and in a sense felt destined to marry Wolff. The subsequent degradation she fell into can be attributed in part to her learning about the wife and child Wolff had left behind on Earth.) Ripple asserts that Wolff's decision to return to Earth was motivated by the broken engagement with Lynn-Minmei. Wolff was suddenly convinced that he could take up where he had left off with the family he had abandoned. When that didn't occur, he turned to drink and drugs and embarked on a campaign of self-destruction. (Information that has only recently come to light suggests that Wolff also had a brief affair with Dana Sterling—the daughter of Max and Miriya, who took Wolff's ship back into space with the hyperdrive perfected by her former Southern Cross comrade, Dr. Louie Nichols—and that Wolff had learned the Invid were holding hostage both his wife Catherine and his son Johnny.)

Selig Kahler, *The Tirolian Campaign*

A WEEK OF HARD RIDING BROUGHT DRAMATIC changes in both the terrain and the social climate of the settlements the team passed through. The land was thickly forested except where it had been cleared for farm cooperatives and villages. The road system was well maintained, and food and supplies were readily available. Lunk knew the reason for this: They were approaching one of the Invid's so-called Protoculture farms, where Human laborers were forced to toil endlessly in vast gardens, maintaining and harvesting the aliens' nutrient plant, the Flower of Life. But where the team had expected to encounter armies of Scouts and Troopers, they found none; and in place of a downtrodden populace, they found people in a celebratory mood. The Invid were said to have stopped their patrols a little over a month ago, and there were rumors to the effect that this had something to do with the arrival of a platoon of Robotech soldiers who were currently engaged in an assault on the Protoculture farm itself.

Scott was certain this unit was composed of men and women from the Mars Division attack wing. One of the predesignated rendezvous points set up by the mission commander was located some five hundred miles north of the team's present coordinates, and it was likely that a splinter group from the main force had moved south to engage the Invid at the farm. Scott was tempted to take the Alpha north to see for himself, but his sense of loyalty wouldn't permit leaving his friends on their own. At least not until each of them had found a peace of sorts or, better still, a home. It was no secret to any of them that the team was more like a family than the invincible military machine each member sometimes imagined it to be. And it was something none of them took for granted, least of all Scott, the most recent victim of the war's dispassionate savagery.

So they stayed together and eventually found their way to the city where the Robotech soldiers were supposedly garrisoned. It was an immense place, far larger than any of the places they had passed through thus far, a former military base (whose buildings had been adapted for civilian use) that had grown up within the confines of an enormous depression in the Earth's denuded crust, enclosed by the severe walls of an unnatu ral escarpment. The city now had hotels, restaurants, and a thriving population of five thousand or more.

Scott left the Alpha concealed outside the city and rode down into the bowl with Lancer and the others. As newcomers, they were questioned and searched at the main gate—an immense security fence watched over by armed guards stationed in nearby ultratech towers—but ultimately permitted to enter.

Scott, already searching for familiar faces, was perhaps a bit more hopeful than the others if no less puzzled. There were indeed soldiers all over the place, but they were hardly the strac troops Scott had convinced himself he would find. Nor were they Mars Division. Their high-collared, belted jumpsuits were the same ice-blue color as Scott's own, but the unit patches were unlike any he had seen. Scott glanced around some more, certain he would find what he was after. Here were three soldiers stumbling out of a bar; there, three more drinking on a street corner. Other troops in jeeps and personnel carriers were joyriding through the narrow streets, trash and empty liquor bottles in their wake. Even Annie was stunned.

"What's with this place?" she asked from the van. She was standing on the seat in the open back, her arms draped over the vehicle's roll bar.

"There's no shortage of 'Culture, that's for sure," Rand observed, motioning to the cruising jeeps.

Scott tuned in to a nearby conversation—soldiers, new arrivals by the sound of them: "This town's a gas!" one of them said. "Unbelievable," said another. "I didn't think I could ever feel this way again."

Scott heard tires squeal behind him and turned around. A jeep was accelerating drunkenly from the main gate, slaloming its way up the street, four soldiers laughing it up inside. It pulled up shortly next to Scott, one of the soldiers offering a bottle out of the top.

When Scott refused, the man said: "What's your problem, pal?" His glazed eyes took in the rest of the group. "You guys look like a war's going on."

"What about the Invid, soldier?" Scott snarled. "A couple hits of that stuff and you forget, huh?"

The soldiers looked at one another, speechless for a moment, then laughed. "Where you been, Colonel?" asked the driver. "They're history. We've been kickin' ass and takin' names all over this sector."

"It's no lie," said another. "Long as ya stick 'round here, ya got nothin' to worry 'bout. So, enjoy. The man's got it covered."

"You can get anything you want here, get me?"

"What man? What are you talking about?" Scott yelled as the jeep screeched off.

"At ease, Colonel!" one of them yelled, eliciting laughter from the others.

It was the same scene wherever they went: everyone talking up the town like it was paradise. Drunken soldiers, hookers, scammers, Foragers, rogues, and hustlers, all thrown together in the same pot, reveling and lifting their glasses in toasts to the mystery man who secured all this for them. The search for food and drink led the team into one of the many bars along the strip. Annie's attempt to flirt with the sideburned bartender ended with his walking off just as Lunk was about to order. Lunk was looking around for something to throw at the guy, when a soldier burst in through the bar's swinging doors.

"Wolff's back!" he yelled to the crowd at the top of his lungs.

Almost everyone got the message—out of sheer volume or at mention of the name itself—and many started for the door. Others, too drunk to move, got as far as lifting their heads from various tabletops. Scott took hold of a soldier within reach and spun him around.

"Who's Wolff?" he demanded of the man.

"The Wolff, bro," the man slurred. "*The* Wolff."

"Jonathan Wolff?" said Scott.

The man snapped his fingers, pointed, and winked at Scott, then shuffled off toward the door.

Rand saw the look of disbelief surface on Scott's face, but before he could ask about it, Scott was shoving his way through the exiting crowd and making for the street.

Rand and the others followed Scott out and found him amid a mob that had gathered around a jeep. Scott was standing rigidly by the curb, mouth half-open in amazement, staring at the man who was climbing out from the driver's side of the vehicle. A celebrity, Rand thought. Either that or a Robo officer who fancied himself one. The man was of medium build but square-shouldered and muscular. He had brown hair, thick and combed straight back, well-defined eyebrows, and a mustache, clipped clear in the center. He was wearing dark glasses and a gray uniform offset by a wide black belt and a red ascot. There was, however, something stern and humorless about him that made Rand wonder at the reception he was getting.

People in the crowd were firing questions left and right, some of which Wolff took the time to answer and others he ignored. At the same time, a wounded soldier in the rear of the jeep was singing Wolff's praises. "He saved my life," the man bit out. "Picked me up and carried me on his back through the Invid lines ... then went back for the Protoculture canisters he knew we needed. . . ."

"Celebration time!" yelled a black man behind Rand. "Drinks on the house!"

But Rand heard someone else mutter: "Wolff's a damn hero every time he comes back. How d' ya figure it?"

Scott swung around at the comment, his face dark and

angry, but said nothing. Until he turned back to Jonathan Wolff. Then Rand heard him say: "I can't believe he's alive—*alive*!"

Colonel Jonathan Wolff... Graduated first in his class from the Robotech Academy on Macross Island but missed the SDF-1's inadvertent jump to Pluto and the two-year odyssey that followed. Nevertheless, he had distinguished himself during that period by openly criticizing the Council's decision to turn its back on the fortress's crew and unwitting civilian population and was resolute in his opposition to Russo, Hayes, and Edwards and their plan to use the Grand Cannon against the Zentraedi. He rose to the fore again during the planet's two-year period of reconstruction and was finally handpicked by Admiral Hunter to head up the ground-base division of the Robotech Expeditionary Force.

But it was on Tirol that Wolff's name became legend and his special forces—known by then as the Wolff Pack—rode to glory. Throughout the Tirolian campaign against the Invid, it was Wolff's forces who turned the tide of battle time and time again. And it was Wolff who came to play a crucial part in the schism that all but destroyed the Pioneer Mission.

Even that wasn't enough for the man. Leaving Dr. Lang and his Saturn group in charge of things on Tirol, Wolff had gone off with Hunter and that group of galactic freedom fighters who called themselves the Sentinels. To Spheris, Gáruda, Haydon IV, to every world that had fallen to the Invid, to every world reduced to slave colonies by the Regent and his limitless army of Inorganics.

Then, for reasons few understood, he had volunteered for a more hazardous assignment: to follow in the tracks of Major John Carpenter in attempting to return a warship to the Earth all of them had left behind. An Earth that had been ravaged by the very Tirolian Masters the Pioneer Mission had aimed to disempower and now faced an even greater threat from the race those same Masters had turned savage and indomitable.

Wolff left Tirol, but not before he had saved the life of a young man who idolized him from afar . . . an assistant to the celebrated Dr. Lang named Scott Bernard. . . .

Silently, Scott ran over the facts and memories while waiting for a chance to speak with Wolff. It was incredible enough that the man had made it back from Tirol, given the then primitive state of the hyperdrive units, but for Scott to find him now, after all these years, was nothing less than miraculous.

From what he had managed to piece together since first seeing Wolff earlier in the day, Scott learned that Wolff had arrived on Earth shortly after the destruction of the Robotech Masters' fleet, approximately two years before the arrival of the Invid. His Wolff Pack had led the counteroffensive but had been decimated along with most of the Army of the Southern Cross. But Wolff himself had survived. Driven underground, he had spearheaded the resistance and ever since had been on the go continually, moving from place to place to recruit and reconnoiter, waiting for the moment when the rest of the Expeditionary Force returned to wage the final battle.

Still, the boisterous atmosphere of the town disturbed Scott. Where was the discipline that had made the Pack such a respected outfit? And why weren't the troops being organized for a coordinated assault against Reflex Point? Why, in fact, was Wolff here, so far south of the central hive, and where were the survivors of Mars Division?

Scott had all these things on his mind when he stepped into Wolff's personal quarters that night and offered salute.

"Lieutenant Commander Scott Bernard, Robotech Expeditionary Force, Mars Division."

Wolff was on the bed, his shirt-sleeves rolled up. "Mars Division?" he said, reaching for his dark glasses; then he laughed shortly: "Well, one of you made it through after all."

Scott lowered his hand from his forehead, somewhat stunned. "Then you haven't rendezvoused with any of the survivors, sir?"

Wolff got off the bed and walked over to the bureau. "Lieutenant—Bernard, you said?—you're the first I've seen." When he saw Scott agape, he laughed again. "Welcome to Earth, Lieutenant. Care for a drink?"

Scott declined and watched Wolff pour a tall one for himself. The small room reeked of stale sweat and liquor and was littered with the remains of half-eaten meals and empty bottles. Scott noticed that Wolff's hand shook as he downed the drink.

"Well, let's not stand on ceremony, Bernard," Wolff said exuberantly. "Have a seat. You can tell me about your ill-fated offensive and I'll tell you about mine."

"Sir, I'm not really here to socialize . . ."

"Oh, I see," Wolff said from the couch, with mock seriousness. "What's this about, then?"

Scott stared at the man before replying, fighting an impulse to turn around and leave the room before matters got worse. "You don't remember me, do you, sir? I knew you on Tirol. I was part of the Saturn group, an assistant to Dr. Lang."

Wolff's grin straightened; he turned his face away from Scott. "That was a long time ago, Bernard. And a lot of miles from here." He put the drink glass aside. "I'm sorry about this, Bernard. We lost quite a few good men today. And there's damn few left."

"Sir, about this town . . . The Wolff Pack—"

"This isn't the Wolff Pack, Lieutenant!" Wolff barked.

"The Wolff Pack is dead, every last one of them." He got up and returned to the bottle. "I know what you're thinking, Bernard. That the noble Jonathan Wolff is but a ghost of his former self and that he can't even control his troops. But you don't know the full story, Bernard. Not the half of it!"

Wolff scowled and set the drink aside without tasting it. "These men aren't soldiers—they're rogues and thieves and Foragers and every other kind of riffraff this planet has spawned during the past fifteen years. I do what I can with the few real soldiers I cross paths with. But this is Earth, not Tirol. And our enemy behaves differently here . . . As we all do."

Scott wasn't sure what to say, so he simply came to the point. "I'd like to be part of your team, sir."

Now it was Wolff's turn to stare. "You obviously know what you're in for, Bernard."

"I've fought my way through a thousand miles, if that's what you mean."

Wolff's eyebrows went up behind the dark glasses. "Impressive."

"In fact," Scott said excitedly, "if it's good troops you're looking for—"

"No," Wolff cut him off firmly. "I don't care how good they are. If they're not Robotech-trained, I don't want them." He turned his back to Scott to stare out the window.

"But, sir—"

"That will be all for now, Bernard."

Scott buttoned his lip and saluted. "Your orders?"

"Oh-five-hundred sharp at the main gate," Wolff said without turning around.

Four Cyclone riders suited up in battle armor left the basin base at sunrise, ascended the escarpment, and headed into the lush forests an hour's ride east. Wolff,

Todd, Wilson, and Bernard. Scott had made no mention of his meeting with Wolff to Rand or the others. He had gone as far as bunking with them in a room they had managed to secure in one of the base's barracks turned hotels and had crept out under the cover of darkness after leaving a scrawled note of explanation on his bedroll. He had to admit that it felt strange and discomforting to be without them, his surrogate family and personal "wolf pack." But he told himself it was time to begin distancing himself from them; his new loyalties would have to lie with Wolff and whatever missions lay ahead of them.

The four men left their Cyclones in the woods and followed Wolff's lead along a faint trail that coursed over low hills to an enormous clearing. Through the foliage, Scott caught glimpses of a massive red hemisphere of some sort. It troubled him that they had left the Cyclones behind and were closing on the Invid Protoculture farm armed only with hand weapons. Wolff's explanation made sense—that they wouldn't be able to get near the place on Protoculture-fueled mecha—but even so, it was hard to imagine that simple H–90's could effect much damage.

It was only when they reached the edge of the clearing that Wolff made the rest of the plan clear: It was imperative that they make off with enough Protoculture to fuel the massive rescue operation Wolff was planning. Each previous mission had brought him closer to this goal, and today's could complete the rescue team's requirements. Beyond that, the four of them simply had to keep themselves from being fried by annihilation discs. Scott had a clear view of the farm now and understood why Wolff hadn't attempted to describe the place earlier —it had to be seen to be believed. It was a hemisphere, all right, but one that stood more than three hundred feet high and was nearly a mile in circumference. It was a kind of blood-red, organic-looking geodesic dome, lit from within by a pulsing light. And from its techno-system base extended ten tentaclelike projections, each a good fifty feet around. Scott imagined that it must have resembled a jellyfish creature from above.

Wolff whispered a warning to his men. "Don't be fooled just because you don't see any Invid. They're around, you can be sure of it." Wolff had the faceshield of his Cyclone helmet raised; he had his dark glasses on.

Scott had to admit that the man was cool and alert, not the boozing, self-pitying Wolff he had seen the night before but the Wolff who had led the Pack up the glory road.

"There are two entry points above the foundation. The Protoculture is stored just inside these," Wolff said, gesturing to two arched portals in the membranous portion of the hemisphere wall. He told Todd and Wilson to take the south one. "Bernard and I will take the other one."

The three men nodded.

"Don't overburden yourselves," Wolff added. "Just take what you can carry without weighing yourselves down. Remember, you might need a free hand for those blasters." Wolff grinned. "But I hope it won't come to that."

Wilson and Todd moved off, using one of the tentacles for cover. Wolff waved Scott forward a moment later.

Halfway along one of the segmented tentacles, Wolff and Scott stopped, huddling down with their backs against the thing, waiting for Wilson and Todd to reach the south portal.

But something unexpected occurred just as Wilson was stepping through.

"Wolff!" Scott heard Todd shout over the suit's tac net. "There's a force field of some kind!" He and Wolff turned at the same moment: Wilson seemed to be suspended in the entrance, arms up over his head, his body shaking as energy coursed through his suit. The ground was rumbling all of a sudden, and before they could take a step toward their two comrades, an Invid Trooper erupted from the ground not twenty feet in front of them.

The shock of seeing the thing must have been enough to break the charge that held Wilson, Scott guessed, because now both he and Todd were heading back toward the woods at a run, dodging a pincer swipe along the way. Scott and Wolff adopted a similar tactic, only to find their route back to safety blocked by a second Invid. The Trooper emerged with enough force to throw Scott off his feet.

A third Trooper had cut off Wilson and Todd's retreat as well, and the two men were depleting their blaster charges against it.

Wolff was shouting for Scott to get up, all the while pouring energy from his handgun into the face of the alien. Peripherally, Scott saw a flash of white light and experienced a wave of searing heat; he turned in time to see Wilson and Todd disintegrate beneath a storm of annihilation discs, their death screams a piercing sound track through the net.

Wolff, meanwhile, had managed to chase off the Invid that had been looming over them only a minute before. Scott couldn't figure out how he had pulled it off but didn't stop to question it. He was on his feet now, Wolff's commands to run for it in his ears. The tree line was only fifty feet away, and he made a mad dash for it. . . .

CHAPTER
FIFTEEN

The incident with Jonathan Wolff dealt a severe blow to the team. Not only because the episode touched them more deeply than they thought possible—they were not as inured as they liked to think—but primarily because it seemed to shift the burden of responsibility entirely onto their shoulders: There was no resistance, except for their own meager efforts. But they would get over Wolff's treachery. How could they not, once confronted with the disillusionments that lay ahead?

Zeus Bellow, *The Road to Reflex Point*

THE NOTE SCOTT LEFT FOR THE TEAM ONLY MADE matters worse. It read: "Don't anyone worry. I can't tell you where I'm going or what I'll be doing, but I'll be back around sunset. Scott."

It was the secrecy that troubled Rand most. If Scott had simply disappeared for the day, Rand might not have given his absence a second thought, but when Scott failed to return with Colonel Wolff that afternoon, he and Rook decided to take matters into their own hands. They didn't bother with the formalities of the chain of command that kept Jonathan Wolff insulated from the city's rabble; they simply made their own way to his room and burst in on the man uninvited.

"Where's Scott, Colonel?" Rand said, out of breath from his run down the hall.

Wolff turned puffy eyes to them. He was seated at a table in the fetid room, a half-empty bottle of vodka in front of him. He had barely moved when Rand and Rook had thrown open the door and was now regarding them tiredly, with little concern.

"Scott who?" he said, refilling his glass.

"Bernard," said Rook. "We know he was with you this morning, and he hasn't returned since."

Wolff made a dejected sound and put down his glass. He reached for his dark glasses and slid them on. "Bernard . . ."

"Well?"

Tight-lipped, Wolff turned his gaze from them and shook his head.

Rand gasped. "You mean . . ."

"I can't say for sure. The Invid surprised us, and in the confusion I didn't see if he made it out or not. They were waiting for us, and we were overmatched. What more can I tell you?"

Struggling with the possible truth of it, Rand said nothing. But a suspicious look had begun to surface on Rook's face. "A whole lot more," she told Wolff. "How did you escape, Colonel?"

Wolff shrugged. "I was luckier than the others. That's the way it is."

Rook snorted. "From what I hear, that's the way it always is with you."

"What are you insinuating?" Wolff seethed, flashing her a cold look.

Rand gestured Rook to back off. He took two steps toward the table and slammed his hand down. "Just tell us where you were attacked."

Wolff's hand went out to steady the bottle. "If you're thinking about trying to go out there and find him, forget it. You won't make it."

Rand showed his teeth, then relaxed. "Look, we've

got an Alpha fighter hidden nearby. If there's even a chance that Scott's alive, you better believe I'm going out there to find him."

Mention of the VT seemed to bring Wolff around somewhat. He lifted the bottle but set it down without pouring. "Even a fighter might not be enough." Wolff gave Rand an appraising look. "Yes, Scott told me that you'd seen action together. But we're up against a hive, not a Scout patrol."

"It's still worth a try."

Wolff thought a moment, then said: "All right, I'll lead you out there."

"Great!"

Wolff stood up and went for his jacket. "We'll leave immediately."

Rand swung around to Rook. "Let the others know what I'm up to. We'll get Scott back!"

With that he rushed from the room, Wolff a few paces behind him. Rook stood dumbfounded for a moment, then followed him to the doorway. "What am I—your personal messenger or something?" she yelled to his back. But he didn't turn around. "Rand!" she shouted again, fuming.

Rand showed Wolff where the Alpha was hidden, but the colonel insisted they recon the area on Cyclones before bringing the Veritech into play. The fighter, Wolff insisted, would stir up the entire hive; it was simply too precious a commodity to risk, even for the life of a valued friend.

Rand saw the logic of it, disturbing as it was, especially after Wolff had led him to the hive.

"The place is a fortress!" Rand exclaimed, keeping his voice low. "I've never seen anything like it."

Wolff regarded him from behind the dark glasses, obviously pleased by Rand's shocked reaction. They were at the edge of the clearing now, suited up in Cyclone armor and armed with hand blasters. "It's just one of many," Wolff said. "There's a chain of these things that runs clear to Reflex Point."

Rand swallowed hard, discouraged. "It was around here that you last saw Scott?"

Wolff nodded and lowered the helmet's faceshield. "We'll search the perimeter first." He motioned Rand off to the right. "Stick to the woods, and I'll meet you on the other side. I only hope there's something left of Bernard to find."

Rand refused to allow the thought to register. He turned and was about to move off when the ground began to tremble. Wolff drew his blaster and pivoted through a 360, searching for some sign of the Invid's egress point. Rand managed to get his blaster unholstered and aimed in the same general direction as Wolff's.

In a moment the Invid Trooper showed itself, rising up through the earth and underbrush just outside the clearing. Wolff and Rand hit it full power, but neither of them was successful at directing a charge to any of the creature's vulnerable points. The Trooper seemed to sense their helplessness and opted to kill them with its claw rather than cannon fire. It had one of its pincers raised for a downward strike, when someone behind the two men stunned it with a Scorpion delivered to the head.

Rand turned in time to see Rook's red Cyclone's rear-wheel landing in the clearing. She slid the tail end of the mecha around and shouted through the externals for Rand to jump on.

"I told you you weren't leaving me behind," Rand heard as he raced to the Cyc. "And it's a lucky thing for you two that I decided to follow."

As Rand straddled the Cyclone's rear seat, he realized

that Wolff wasn't behind him. Over his shoulder he glimpsed Wolff waving Rook off. "Get going!" Wolff told them. "I'll make it back to my mecha!"

Rook wasn't about to sit around and argue. She toed the Cyclone into gear and sped off almost before Rand had secured an adequate handhold behind her. Meanwhile, the stunned Invid had come to life and was spewing a horizontal hail of annihilation discs into the trees. The Trooper pursued them, its shoulder cannons blazing. Rook pushed the Cyclone through a series of twists and turns, dodging explosions, plumes of fire and dirt.

Rand was thinking they were in the clear when the carapaced head of a second Invid appeared in front of them, pushing itself up from the soft forest ground, an unearthly land crab. Rook tried to launch the Cyclone over the thing before it completed its rise, but the Invid got one of its pincers free just as the mecha was directly overhead. Rand felt the jolt as the alien's claw impacted the mecha, and the next thing he knew he was on his butt in the grass, dazed, Rook similarly postured nearby. The Cyclone was nowhere in sight.

Rand shook his head clear and raised the helmet faceshield. "We've gotta find the Cyc," he shouted to Rook. "Split up."

Rook got to her feet; Rand waved her the okay sign and disappeared into the brush.

Splitting up was a bad idea, Rand told himself fifteen minutes later. The woods were thick, impenetrable in places; he had started working circles to fix his location, but he soon lost track of his own center—along with Rook and the missing Cyclone.

He was close to the hive clearing again, removing his helmet, when he heard sounds of movement close by. Rand turned, glimpsed Colonel Wolff, and almost called out to him. But something made him pull himself into concealment at the last moment. Wolff had holstered his blaster and looked as though he were waiting for a delivery of some kind. A Human-size figure was walking toward Wolff, but it was still too far off for Rand to get a good look at it. And even when it finally approached Wolff, he didn't know what to make of it.

Rand had his H–90 aimed at the thing now: It was taller than it had first appeared, perhaps eight feet tall, bipedal and suited up in bulky dark-colored battle armor. The creature's head—if that was indeed its head and not some kind of helmet—reminded Rand of a snail's foot. He told himself that it had to be an Invid. It certainly matched Scott's description of them, but Rand had for so long come to think of the aliens' ships as the creatures themselves that his mind refused to accept the idea.

Then Rand saw the Invid soldier hand Wolff a carry pack of Protoculture canisters.

He was tempted to kill them both—alien and traitor —but knew as the rage spread through him that he wanted Wolff to *know* who was taking him out when the moment came.

Rand lowered the weapon and silently began to work his way toward the conspirators. There was an outcropping of rock behind Wolff; Rand made his way to the top of this while the Invid walked back to the hive. Wolff had the Protoculture and was about to return to his Cyclone when Rand surprised him.

"So the hero's a traitor," Rand said from the outcropping, his blaster aimed down at Wolff. Wolff had been quick to raise his own weapon, but Rand went on, undaunted. "No wonder the city's full of laughing soldiers —it's so safe and secure now that you've arrived."

Rand risked a leap and in a moment was standing face to face with Wolff, who had yet to say a word. "The Robotech hero's made a deal with the Invid! For a few measly canisters of Protoculture, the great Jonathan Wolff leads his own soldiers to the Invid's doorstep. Isn't that it?"

Wolff fired.

The low-charge blast caught Rand in the right forearm guard, knocking the weapon from his grip and sending a jolt of searing heat to the flesh beneath the battle armor. He went down on one knee, as much from surprise as pain, and stared up at Wolff in disbelief.

"Go ahead and finish me," Rand spat. "I was meant to be Invid bait anyway...Just like Scott and all the others.... It's how you always manage to return in one piece and well stocked with 'Culture...."

Wolff put the short muzzle of the blaster to Rand's head. "Easy, boy," he warned him.

Rand was shaking uncontrollably in spite of his best efforts to contain his fear. "How could you do it?" he asked Wolff. "Scott idolized you.... He told me you'd saved his life once."

"Now you know about the dark side of heroism," Wolff said flatly.

Rand could feel the blaster's priming charge grounding on his skull. He wished he could see the man's eyes, know just what he was thinking. "I've seen it before— everyone out to save their own necks, trading lives... But why you, Wolff? Why?"

Wolff retracted the blaster. "Because they can't be beaten." He sneered. "Because it's better to have a few safe towns than an entire planet of slaves...And because...because of things you wouldn't understand, kid."

Rand scowled. "You better kill me, Wolff, because I'm gonna see to it that you're stopped."

Wolff stepped back and holstered his sidearm. "Go ahead and tell the town. See if they believe you."

Wolff turned and hurried off.

* * *

Rand unfastened the scorched battle armor from his forearm while he watched Wolff leave. Relieved that his burns weren't as serious as he had feared, he began to search the tall grass and brush for his blaster, wondering if he might be able to catch up with Wolff before he reached the Cyclones.

Go ahead and tell the town, Rand recalled Wolff telling him. *See if they believe you.*

Suddenly he heard Rook's voice and looked up. Scott was with her, one arm draped over Rook's shoulders for support. His battle armor was blackened in places, but he looked otherwise intact.

"I can't believe my eyes," Rand said, extending his hand to Scott. "Is it really you?"

"Barely," Scott returned.

"I found him in a hole in the ground." Rook laughed.

"And I miss it already." Scott disengaged himself from Rook and started to say something about a prehistoric-looking creature he had seen while in hiding, when he spied Wolff several hundred yards off. He tried a shaky step in that direction and said to Rand, "Is that Colonel Wolff? He came back to look for me?"

Rand put a hand out to restrain him. "Let him go, Scott." Scott looked over his shoulder, puzzled. "I've got something to tell you, and you're not going to like it . . . Wolff . . . Wolff's a traitor. He's got an arrangement with the Invid—he's been trading soldiers' lives for Protoculture."

"What are you talking about?" Scott's eyes were flashing.

"He's a traitor! I saw him with my own eyes. And an Invid, Scott, not a ship but—"

Rand didn't see the punch coming. Now, lying face-down in the grass, he couldn't even remember feeling it. "You're lying, you little coward!" Scott was yelling.

Rand rolled over and sat up, feeling a slight numbness beginning to spread across his jaw. "When I confronted him, he didn't deny it. I'm telling you, we were both led out here to be killed."

Scott roared something and launched himself, but Rook stepped in his way. In his weakened state he was no match for Rook and was easily held back. But she could do nothing about the curses he was hurling Rand's way.

All at once a fiery explosion effectively erased all traces of the struggle, the concussive force of it flattening Rook and Scott to the grass on either side of Rand. Through the smoke the three could see Trooper after Trooper issuing from the ground around them, blinding globes of incipient fire at the tips of shoulder cannons.

In a moment, annihilation discs were zipping into the area, pulverizing rocks and roots and whatever else lay in their path. Rand helped Scott make it to the safety of the stone outcropping, while Rook laid down cover fire with her hand blaster.

"The Cyclones—where are they?!" said Scott.

Rook indicated a direction. "I'll see if I can slow these things down some. Swing back around and pick me up."

Scott and Rand signaled their assent and rushed off, crouching as they ran.

Jonathan Wolff watched them from another part of the forest. He was surprised to see that Bernard had lived and was strangely relieved. Nevertheless, his escape had been but a minor stay of execution, for there were at least six Troopers going up against the three freedom fighters. Wolff could see that the woman was remaining behind to buy time for her comrades. But even if the other two were fortunate enough to make it to their Cyclones, it would just be a matter of time.

Unless someone came to their aid with the appropriate firepower.

An Alpha fighter, for instance, Wolff said to himself.

Rand got to the Cyclone first and doubled back to pick up Rook and convey her to the waiting red. Afterward he launched and went to Battle Armor mode, neatly disposing of one of the Troopers with a single shot to the thing's sensor.

Rook and Scott were similarly reconfigured now and going after a second alien. Scott dazzled the Trooper with in-close fancy flying, then boosted up and away from its pincer swipes to loose a Scorpion, which the creature blocked with its claw armor. In return the Invid pilot loosed a volley of annihilation discs against Scott, but in so doing had overlooked Rook and the missile she launched straight to its vulnerable scanner. The Trooper was blown to pieces, and the three teammates regrouped on the ground. The woods around them were crawling with Invid.

"We're surrounded," Rand thought to point out, his back to Rook and Scott. "Now what do we do?"

"What we always do," said Scott, almost laughing. "Fight our way out. Now, look alive."

Rand launched first, but critically misjudged his trajectory and ended up snagged by a Trooper's claw. Scott heard his desperate cry through the net, but even before he could think about how to free his friend, a bolt out of the blue took the Invid's pincer off at the elbow. An instant later, Scott saw the Alpha streak overhead. He was confused until he heard Rand yell, "Wolff! It's gotta be him!"

Wolff had the VT in Guardian mode. Missiles tore from undercarriage launch tubes, detonating like geysers of fire around one of the Troopers. But the creature survived the storm and struck back. Wolff rolled and tumbled the fighter through a steady stream of discs and dropped in to knock the troublemaker off its feet. He then switched to Battloid mode and came back down at the rest of them, the rifle/cannon discharging white death from its high-port position.

There were two Pincer ships in the skies now, and Wolff propelled the Alpha up to deal with them. One of the Invid had barely arrived in the arena when it was disintegrated by a flock of heat-seekers Wolff launched from the Battloid's shoulder racks.

On the ground, Scott was saying, "A traitor wouldn't handle an Alpha like that." He and the others had followed the fight and were now in the arid heights west of the base escarpment.

Wolff came on the net a moment later. "Just thought I'd give you a few pointers, flyboy."

"Be my guest!" Scott enthused.

Wolff kept the VT in Battloid configuration to take out the second Pincer ship before moving against the remaining Troopers. He literally stomped one of these senseless by bringing the mecha down full force on the alien's head. But the acrobatic act ended up costing him a precious few seconds: Wolff pivoted the Battloid in time to deal with the final Invid, but not before the Trooper succeeded in holing the techno-knight with an energy bolt that passed clear through it like a flaming spear.

Scott watched the crippled Battloid go down on one knee, then reconfigure to Guardian mode, seemingly of its own accord.

"Colonel Wolff!" he yelled, running over to the fighter. "Are you all right?"

The canopy went up, and Wolff managed to clamber out of the cockpit, one hand pressed to his side wound. He lowered himself to the ground, collapsing into Scott's arms. Gently, Scott laid Wolff on the ground, his own hands now awash in the colonel's blood. "You're bleeding, sir," he told Wolff hurriedly. "We've got to get you back to the base."

Wolff reached up and removed his dark glasses. "Too late, Bernard," he answered weakly, eyes closed. "Get yourselves out of here on the double."

"I won't let you die like this," Scott objected. "You're coming back with us!"

Wolff forced his eyes open and looked hard into Scott's own. "I'm a traitor, Commander—"

"Colonel—"

"And a traitor should be left to die out in the open..." Wolff shivered from a cold that began deep down in his guts. "When I think of the lives I traded to save my own skin..." Wolff screamed as something seemed to come loose inside him. Scott watched him blanch and felt the dying man's grip tighten on his arm.

"Colonel, hang on—"

"Catherine...Johnny...*Minmei*!" Wolff gasped, and died.

Scott shut the dead man's eyes, stood up, and saluted. In the distance he could see Lunk and Annie bounding toward the Alpha in the van. Alongside them rode Lancer on a Cyclone he had probably picked up at the base.

Scott looked over his shoulder at Rook and Rand; they looked back at him blankly, drained of emotion. Scott wondered whether they felt the same confusion he did. Gazing down at Wolff's body, gazing out at the smoldering remains of half a dozen Invid ships, he asked himself how this war could ever be won.

Or if indeed a war like this could ever have winners.

He thought about the long road ahead of them—his team, his family. Would it be as bloodstained a journey as these past few months? *Marlene*, he said to himself, reflexively reaching for the holo-locket around his neck.

To go through all this and yet never be able to win back your life!

The following chapter is a sneak preview of METAMORPHOSIS—Book XI in the continuing saga of ROBOTECH.

> *How could so many of the principals in this vast struggle be so blind to the reason that one planet was at the center of it all? That is a secret we shall never know.*
>
> *On blighted Earth, arguably the most warlike planet in the Universe, the Flower of Life had taken root like nowhere else before—except for Optera (which may or may not have been its world of origin). And in so doing, it set the stage for Act III of the Robotech Wars.*
>
> *And yet, inventively oblivious, Invid and Human alike attributed that to the vagaries of a plant.*
>
> Zeus Bellow, *The Road to Reflex Point*

NEVER HAS THE *FLOWER OF LIFE* WROUGHT MORE *strangely!* it occurred yet again to the Regis, empress/ mother of the Invid species. *Earth, your fate is wedded to ours now!*

How strange it was that Zor had chosen Earth, she thought, as she poised there in the center of the stupendous mega-hive know as Reflex Point. Or, more aptly, how *well* he had chosen by sending his dimensional fortress to the planet so long ago. Of all the worlds that circled stars, what had made him pick this one? The thought of Zor made her seethe with a passion that had long since turned to austere hatred.

Did he know that Earth would prove so fantastically fertile for the Flowers of Life, a garden second only to the Invid race's native Optera in its receptivity to the Flowers? It was true that Protoculture could bestow powers of mind, but even so, what had drawn Zor's attention across the endless light-years to the insignificant blue-white globe?

But Zor's decision didn't matter now. All that was important was that the Invid had finally found a world where the all-important Flower thrived. At long last, they had conquered their New Optera.

Of course, there was an indigenous species—the Human race—but they did not present any problem. The first onslaught of the Invid had left Human civilization in ruins; the aliens used many of the survivors to farm the Flower of Life.

A few Humans cowered in and around the shattered remains of their cities, or prowled the wastelands, preying on one another and dreading the moment when the Invid would finish the job. The only use in letting the Homo sapiens survive a little while longer was to use them to further the Invid master plan.

Then, the Humans would be sent into oblivion forever. There was no room for them on Earth any more. And from what the Regis knew of the Human race's history, their absence would improve the universe as a whole.

And it *would* be done. After all, the last of the Regis's real enemies were dead. There was no one to oppose the might of the undefeated and remorseless Invid.

The Alpha fighter bucked, but cut a clean line through the air, its drives flaring blue. Wickedly fast, heavily armed, and hugging the ground, it arrowed toward the snowcapped mountains.

Lieutenant Scott Bernard eased back on his HOTAS —the Hands-on-Throttle-and-Stick controls. With so much power at his disposal, it was tempting to go for speed, to exercise the command of the sky that seemed like the Robotech fighter's birthright, his own.

One reason *not* to speed on ahead was that there were others below, following along in surface vehicles —his team members. It would take them days, perhaps weeks, to cover mountain terrain he could cross in a few minutes. And he didn't dare leave them too far behind; his Alpha was the team's main edge against Invid hunter/killer patrols. The Alpha slowed until it was at near-stalling speed, its thrusters holding it aloft.

Another reason not to give in to the impulse to roar triumphantly across heaven was the fact that Humans *didn't* own the sky anymore.

He opened his helmet mike. "This is Alpha One to Scout Reconnaissance."

A young male voice came back over the tac net, wry and a bit impatient. "I hear you, Scott. What's on your mind?"

Scott controlled his temper. No point in another argument with Rand about proper commo procedure, at least not now.

"I'm about ten miles ahead of you," Scott answered. "We'll never be able to make those mountains before nightfall. I'm turning back; we'll rendezvous and set up camp."

He looked wistfully toward the mountains. There was so far to go, such a long, perilous journey, between here and Reflex Point. And what would be waiting there? The battle for Earth itself, the showdown of the Robotech Wars. The destruction of the greatest stronghold of the Invid realm.

But this group of oddly met guerrillas and a stranded Mars Division fighter pilot were not the Earth's sole saviors. And soon, soon...the demonic Invid would be swept away before a purging storm of Robotechnology.

He increased speed and took the Alpha through a bank, watchful for any sign of Invid war mecha that might have detected the fighter's Protoculture emissions. The fighter complained a bit; he would have to give its systems a thorough going-over with Lunk, the band's tech straw boss.

Scott was less proficient at flying in atmosphere than he would have liked. He had grown up on the SDF-3 expedition and most of his piloting had been done in vacuum. There was an ineffable beauty, a *rightness*, to flying in Earth's atmosphere, but there were also hidden dangers, especially for a combat flier.

Still, he didn't complain. Things were going better than he had expected. At least the supplies of ordnance and Protoculture Scott's team had lifted from the supply depot of the turncoat Colonel Wolff would last them for a while.

Now all they needed was some luck. Somewhere, Scott's Mars Division comrades were getting ready for the assault. Telemetry had told him that a good part of the Mars Division had survived the orbital combat action and planetary approach in which his squadron had been shot to pieces, leaving him the only survivor. Scott still lived with the sights and sounds of those few horrible minutes, as he lived with memories even more difficult to endure.

Reflex Point waited. There the Invid would be repaid a millionfold—an eye for an eye.

From high overhead, Reflex Point resembled a monstrous spiderweb pattern. The joining lines, glowing yellow-red as though they were canals of lava, were formed by Protoculture conduits and systemry. The accessways were traveled by mecha, and by the Regis's other servants.

At the center was the enormous Hive Nucleus that

was Reflex Point proper. It was a glowing hemisphere with a biological look to it, and a strange foam of bubble-like objects around its base like a concentric wave coming in from all sides. The Nucleus was more than twelve miles in diameter. To Human eyes it might have resembled a superhigh-speed photograph of the first instant of an exploding hydrogen bomb. At the various junctures were the lesser domes and instrumentality nodes, though some of those were two miles across.

Deep within Reflex Point, at its center, was a globe of pure Protoculture instrumentality. This veined bronze sphere, with darker shadows moving and Shaping within it, responded to the will of the Regis. A bolt of blazing light broke from the dark vastness overhead, to create an enormous Protoculture bonfire. The Regis spoke and all her children, her farflung species, listened; there was so much to tell them. With the incredible profusion of Flowers of Life that the Earth had provided, the Regis's children had increased in number, and the newly quickened drone zygotes must be instructed in their destiny. From within the huge globe, her will reached forth to manipulate the leaping Protoculture flames. "The living creatures of this world have evolved into a truly amazing variety of types and sub-types."

Images formed in the flames: spider, platypus, swan, rat, Human female. "Many of these are highly specialized, but extremely successful. Others are generalized and adaptable and many of those, too, are successful.

"Earth is the place the Flower of Life has chosen to prosper, and that is a fact that brooks no argument. And so it is the place where the Invid, too, shall live forever. For this, we must find the ultimate life form suitable to our existence here, and assume that form."

All across her planetary domain and among the stars beyond, the Invid stopped to listen. A few could remember the days long ago on Optera, before Zor, when the Invid lived contented and joyous lives. Other, younger Invid had access to those days, too, through the racial memory that was a part of the Regis's power.

On Optera, by ingesting the Flowers of Life, the Invid had experimented with self-transformation and with explorations in auto-evolution that were part experiment, part religious rite. And, with the power of the Protoculture and its Shapings, they strove to peer beyond the present and the visible, into the secrets of the universe —into transcendent planes of existence.

Those days were gone, though they would come again when the Flowers covered the New Optera—Earth. For the moment though, evolution would be determined and enacted by the Regis.

"In order to select the ultimate form, the form we will assume for our life here, we are utilizing Genesis Pits for our experiments in bioengineering."

More shadows formed in the otherworldly bonfire. "We have cloned creatures from all significant eras of this planet's history, and are studying them for useful traits at locations all across the globe. We will also study their interaction with the once-dominant species, *Homo sapiens*."

Her disembodied voice rose, ringing like an anthem, stirring Invid on every rung of her species' developmental ladder, from the crudest amoeboid drone-gamete to her most evolved Enforcer.

"Long ago, the Invid made the great mistake of believing alien lies; of believing in trust, of taking part in—" Her voice faltered a little; this final sin had been the Regis's alone.

"In love."

And the love Zor had drawn from her had been mirrored by her male mate, the Regent, as psychotic hatred and loathing. This had caused the Regent to fling himself —purposely and perversely—down and down a de-evolutionary path to monstrousness and mindlessness, to utter amorphous primeval wrath.

The Regis steeled herself. Her mind-voice rang out again.

"But we have paid for those failures for an age! For an age of wandering, warfare, death, and privation! And once we have discovered the Ultimate Form appropriate to this planet, we shall assume that form, and we will secure our endless new supply of the Flower of Life. Our race will become the supreme power it was meant to be!"

But she shielded from her universe of children the misgiving that was never far from her thoughts. Here, on Earth—the planet the Flower *itself* had chosen—the once-dominant life form was cast in the image of Zor.

And again the Regis felt herself fractured in a thousand ways, yet drawn in one direction. *What affliction is more accursed than love?*

Rand bent over the handlebars of his Cyclone combat cycle as Annie yelled, her face pressed close so he could hear her over the mecha's roar and the passage of the wind, and the dampening effect of his Robotech armor.

"Look, there's Scott, at ten o'clock!"

Rand had already seen the hovering blue and white Alpha settling for a VTOL setdown. There weren't many useful-size clearings in the thick forest in this region. Certainly, there was nothing like a suitable airstrip for a conventional fighter craft within a hundred miles or more.

The designers who had given the fighter Vertical Take-off and Landing capability of course knew how important that would be in a tactical situation in a conventional war. But Rand sometimes wondered if they had foreseen how helpful the VTOL would be to a pack of exhausted guerrillas who were Earth's last committed fighting unit.

"I see 'im," Rand yelled back to Annie, rather than point out that he had been tracking Scott both by eye and on the Cyc's display screen. Rand didn't like to admit it, but he had developed a soft spot in his heart for the winsome, infuriating bundle of adolescent energy who had insisted on being part of the team.

Annie had insisted on coming along with him on point, too. She was *determined* to do her share, take her risks, be considered an adult part of the team. Rand saw that a lot of her self-esteem was riding on the outcome, and grumblingly admitted that he wouldn't mind some company. Scott and the rest had given in, perhaps for the same reason that they never questioned the pint-size redhead's outrageous claim that she was all of sixteen.

You could either accept Annie for her feisty self, or risk shattering the brave persona she had forged, with little help or support, to make her way in a dangerous, despair-making world.

Now she banged Rand's armor. "Turn there, turn there!"

"Pillion-seat driver," Rand growled, but he turned down the game path, the cycle rolling slowly, homing in on Scott's signal. "We're about ten minutes ahead of the others, Scott."

Scott's voice came back over the tactical net. "Good. Still no sign of the Invid, but we can run a sweep of the area before the others get here."

None of them saw or registered it on their instruments, but in the dim forest darkness, massive ultratech shapes moved—two-legged, insectlike walking battleships.

Like looming monsters from a madman's nightmare.

ABOUT THE AUTHOR

Jack McKinney has been a psychiatric aide, fusion-rock guitarist and session man, worldwide wilderness guide, and "consultant" to the U.S. Military in Southeast Asia (although they had to draft him for that).

His numerous other works of mainstream and science fiction—novels, radio and television scripts —have been written under various pseudonyms.

He currently resides in Dos Lagunas, El Petén, Guatemala.

ROBOTECH™
The Sentinels

In 2020, members of Earth's Robotech Defense Force decided to send a secret mission to the Robotech homeworld to try to make peace with the Robotech Masters. This mission, led by Rick Hunter and Lisa Hayes, set forth aboard the SDF-3 and spent years in space. Meanwhile, back on Earth, the Robotech Wars continued unabated—and everyone wondered what fate befell the people on the SDF-3, now known as The Sentinels.

It has remained a mystery...until now! For the first time, the full story of the SDF-3 Expeditionary Force is about to be told. At last... the story you have been waiting for is

COMING IN APRIL
from
DEL REY BOOKS

ROBOTECH™